No Enemy

BOOKS BY

FORD MADOX FORD

NO ENEMY

IT WAS THE NIGHTINGALE

PARADE'S END

THE GOOD SOLDIER

PROVENCE

ETC.

No Enemy

by Ford Madox Ford

THE ECCO PRESS

NEW YORK

First published by The Ecco Press in 1984
18 West 30th Street, New York, N.Y. 10001
Published simultaneously in Canada by
George J. McLeod Limited, Toronto
Printed in the United States of America
Library of Congress Cataloging in Publication Data
Ford, Ford Madox, 1873-1939.
No enemy.
Reprint. Originally published: New York:
The Macaulay Co., 1929.
I. Title
PR6011.053N58 1984 823'.912 84-6090
ISBN 0-88001-062-2 (pbk.)

To

ESTHER JULIA MADOX FORD

Très, très chère petite Princesse,

When you shall come to read English—which I hope will not be too soon—you shall find here adumbrated what the world seemed like to me just when you were preparing to enter it . . . . . a confused old world which your coming rendered so much clearer and dearer. And as these pages were written in the expectation of you—and for you!—I have thought better to leave them exactly as they were, bearing as they obviously do the traces of sufferings that, thank God, you never knew. And so, when you come to read them, give a tender thought to him to whom you have so often written—quitoubliejamé et qui t'aime de tou son coeur et encore beaucoupluss!

F. M. F.

NEW YORK, 21st June, 1929

What is love of one's land? . . . .
                                        I don't know very well.
It is something that sleeps
For a year, for a day,
For a month—something that keeps
Very hidden and quiet and still
And then takes
The quiet heart like a wave,
The quiet brain like a spell,
The quiet will
Like a tornado—and that shakes
The whole of the soul.

CONTENTS

Part One—Four Landscapes

Part Two—Certain Interiors

PART ONE

FOUR LANDSCAPES

I

To Introduce Gringoire

THE writer's friend Gringoire, originally a poet and Gallophile, went to the war. Long, gray, lean, unreasonably boastful as a man and unreasonably modest as a poet, he was probably not too disciplined as an infantry officer, but he has survived to inhabit in tranquillity with the most charming of companions a rural habitation so ancient, frail and unreal that it is impossible to think of it otherwise than as the Gingerbread Cottage you may have read of in the tale of "Haensel and Gretel."

This book, then, is the story of Gringoire just after . . . Armageddon. For it struck the writer that you hear of the men that went, and you hear of what they did when they were There. But you never hear how It left them. You hear how things were destroyed, but seldom of the painful processes of Reconstruction.

So that your Compiler, taking pencils, tablets and erasers and availing himself of the singularly open hospitality of the poet and his charming meridional partner, came on many successive Saturday afternoons from the little old Grammar School where he instructs classes in English Literature and Physical Development, to sit in the garden at the feet of Gringoire, Gallophile, Veteran, Gardener and, above all, Economist, if not above all Poet.

We would sit about on rude benches whilst Mme. Sélysette would bring us shandygaff brewed after a recipe of Gringoire himself. Then he would talk and your Compiler make furtive shorthand notes. Above all Gringoire loved to talk about cooking for he boasted that he was not only the best but the most economical cook in the world. How that may be your Compiler hesitates to say. To eat a meal prepared by Gringoire was certainly an adventure and when you felt adventurous had its titillations. But only Mme. Sélysette who had accompanied him into his English wilds from the distant South could have told you whether Gringoire was as economical in his cuisine as he professed to be. For he swore that the saviour of society in the end would be the good but excellently economical cook.

But Mme. Sélysette, dark, alert and with exquisitely

pencilled brows and as loyal as she was goodhumored, never got beyond saying that in his culinary furies Gringoire needed at least three persons—whom I took to be herself, the diminutive maid and the almost more diminutive stable boy—to clear up after he had boiled an egg.

How Gringoire proposed to save the world by intensive kitchen gardening and exquisite but economical cookery may appear hereafter. His years in the trenches had taught him one thing—to be an eccentric economist, *in petto,* since he regarded himself as an extinct poet and proposed to live on his minute army pension. And I think his ambition really was to teach persons forced to live on minute incomes how to lead graceful, poetic and pleasant lives and so to save the world.

Thus it would perhaps have been better could your Compiler have provided you with a work useful to young couples contemplating matrimony on ten shillings a week . . . or a month . . . or a year. That would have been an enterprise certainly to gladden the heart of Gringoire. Or it might have been better had it taken the form of a Cottager Cookery Book or a Cottager's Guide to Gardening or the Keeping of Goats instead of the war-reminiscences of a contemplative and sensitive soul. Yes, to be sure that would have been better. One can only console one's self that when it comes to war-reminiscences the contemplative and sensitive soul has been little represented. So, for the matter of that, has the poetic but economical chef.

But the present writer, alas, has not the excellent—but *so* meticulous!—mind that will let him sit down and write *many* paragraphs such as that following this one. Neither has Gringoire the patience to dictate to the writer details of his methods. The most he has done is to let his Boswell into his frame of mind. We once, together, got as far as this:

"Chops, Mutton, to deal with.

"Fritto Misto: Stock: Mixed Meats *en casserole.*

"Take two chops. Pare off *all* the fat till you have two *noisettes de mouton.* Save each particle of meat and each particle of fat from the tail ends of the chops, separate, but as zealously as you preserve every memory of your well-beloved. You will then have four little divisions: two *noisettes* for the *Fritto Misto;* two chop bones for stock; a little pile of fat for rendering down; a little pile of fragments of meat. Place the bones immediately in a small casserole of water, with salt, two bay leaves, pepper, one leaf of sage, and rice if you like. It will help you if you tie the bones together with a piece of string having a long end so that you may pull them out. Let this simmer for thirty-six hours.[1] Have ready also six roots of salsify; one-half pound of French beans; one-half pound of cooked peas; and one pound of potatoes, cut into slices. (All these vegetables should be cooked ready. It will improve matters if the peas are *very* young and boiled in syrup.) Also two tomatoes sliced in halves, the meat of two rashers of bacon, and a few mushrooms, and half a dozen sprigs of parsley. (The bacon fat must be saved for rendering down.) Also two slices of bread half an inch thick. Have ready also a large pie dish half filled with water.

"Now take an earthenware frying pan with a white glazed lining. Put in sufficient frying fat to fill this to three-quarters of its depth when boiling. Set this on the fire and bring the fat to the boil. (Boiling fat will be absolutely still—stiller than any waters at even; as still as is Madame Sélysette when, in the same room, Gringoire is writing. It will have ceased to bubble, and,

[1] This is the result of the Army. I do not believe that Gringoire ever simmers his bones for thirty-six hours. But in the Army it was woe to the Colonel whose bones did not simmer for thirty-six hours or who did not say so when an apoplectic gentleman with a blue hat-band came around. The Colonel would lose his battalion, his D.S.O., and the esteem of his fellow men.

above its surface, will float a filmy wreath of bluish vapor. You may test it by dropping in a piece of bread crumb. If this becomes crisp in sixty seconds, your fat will be ready for what follows.)

"As soon as the fat boils, drop in your two slices of bread, which will be large enough later to support the *noisettes* and which will be trimmed to improve their appearance. During that minute, place in a frying basket your two *noisettes* of mutton and the sliced cold potatoes. (Gringoire likes his fried potatoes not too crisp. Those who like them biscuit-wise should fry them in the basket for a quarter of an hour longer than the mutton.) Take out from the frying fat the slices of bread, let them drip into the fat, place them handy on a clean plate . . . *D—n it, that's enough!"*

The reader will understand that at this point my friend Gringoire ceased dictating and ceased violently. Thus a Gringoire cookery book cannot be compiled. For, though Gringoire will cook for hours and hours if visitors are expected, and though he will talk, equally for hours and hours, about eating, about digestion, about French, Italian, and even German cookery as they affect the emotions, he finds it tiresome to tie down his mind to the recording of processes.

It is the same with gardening; the keeping of goats, ducks, chickens; the training of dogs, cats, and horses. He will spend hours in meditating over his onion bed.

And then Madame Sélysette will call from the bedroom window of the Gingerbread Cottage:

"I do *love* to see you, Gringoire, pottering about and pretending to be busy." For Gringoire will have risen at 6:30 and will have done something with hoes, spades, trowels, lines, and other paraphernalia. But he will have thought more. For the rotation of crops on a quarter of an acre of sandy soil that has to be at once a formal garden and the main food supply of a couple, of the tiniest income—that is a subject for endless thought.

It is a subject also for endless economies, schemes, calculations. The calculations concern manure—for the accounts of agriculture are the most complicated of accounts. You may show a loss on the fattening of an ox, a chicken, a goat, a duck, or a pig—and yet its droppings may so enrich your land as to give you actually a handsome balance of profit. Or again a crop may appear superabundant, little palatable, or unattractive—but, fed to one animal or another, it will beautifully adorn your board on Christmas day.

So in the Gingerbread Cottage—and it is, in all but looks, a very bad cottage, with a roof that leaks, walls that used to drip with damp, cupboards that, till the advent of Gringoire, smelled of mold and bred the very largest spiders that can be imagined—Gringoire pursues at once his economies, his meditations, and his career as a poet.

But he is only able to be communicative as to his meditations. If Madame Sélysette asks him how to make *potage* this or that, he says: "Oh, throw in any old thing." Or again! This spring the writer overheard the following dialogue between him and a small boy who was weeding whilst he dug.

"What is the most important thing in gardening, boy?"

"Manure, sir."

"What is the next most important thing?"

"Tools, sir."

"And the next?"

"Money to buy seeds, sir."

"Wrong in every particular," said Gringoire in a terrible voice. "The first thing is brains; and the second thing is brains; and the third thing is brains. Do you understand?"

The boy said, "Yes, sir." But one may doubt if he was really much wiser. And Gringoire continued somewhat as follows: "I have no manure, no tools, and no money—but you will see in the autumn that I shall have the most productive garden in the country!"

From which it will appear that Gringoire has some of the characteristics of a Southern origin. Today his garden would not at all points impress a French gardener—but in some it would. For, in his youth Gringoire sat under the great Professor Gressent, Professor of the Potager Moderne, at the Sorbonne in Paris. From him he learned that thought, devotion to the task, and any bit of metal on the end of a stick shaped like a hoe will take the place of manure, tools, and money. For Professor Gressent, during one session, used to commence every lecture by ordering his pupils to inscribe on their tablets the mystical sentence: *"Trois fois biner vaut deux fois engraisser."*

And when his Boswell, the writer, asked him the other day how he got his results, he answered:

"By trying to establish what that old fool Tolstoi called the Kingdom of God within me!"

The writer took him to mean that it is the spirit in which a job is attacked that alone can sanctify the job—and that, in that way, the godly grow fat at the expense of the unrighteous. Before the war Gringoire was an ordinary poet, such as you might see in Soho or in various foreign underground haunts by the baker's dozen, eating nasty meats, drinking nasty wines, usually in nasty company. How the war changed his heart is here recorded.

This is therefore a Reconstructionary Tale.

II

Gardens and Flats

"I WONDER," Gringoire [1] began one evening, "if my experience of landscape during the war has been that of many people. . . ."

It was an evening in spring. Gringoire had not been very long established in his cottage—which, because of the nature of the poet himself and of the poet's adventurous establishment, the writer automatically styles in his mind the Gingerbread Cottage. Gringoire, with a spirit of hospitality that was large and open rather than either considered or calculating, had invited a party of London friends to share his Easter with him. During the day he rushed about a great

[1] "Gringoire." This is not of course, our poet's name, but a nickname earned actually at school. There is a story by Alphonse Daudet, in "Lettres de Mon Moulin," called the "Chèvre de M. Séguin," which relates how in the end the wolf ate Mr. Séguin's goat. This story, in the form of a letter, is addressed to a poet, one Gringoire, and is meant to show that though a poet may struggle all his life against poverty, in the end the wolf, starvation, will get him. At Gringoire's school the Sixth Form were studying French from the "Lettres de Mon Moulin," and since even at that date Gringoire wrote poems, his kindly schoolmates learned the name and so bestowed it upon him—as it has been bestowed on many out-at-elbowed literati.

deal, cooking highly flavored dishes of a ragout type, on paraffin stoves, washing up, sweeping, gardening, gathering unusual wild herbs for salads, so that he was busy, and we of the party saw little of him.

Fortunately it was fine. For at that date the Gingerbread Cottage let in water like a sieve through the roof, the floor, the rough walls. Great holes indeed gaped in the plaster of the ceilings. But he had whitewashed the walls, stuck pots on shelves, improvised a couch out of his camp bed, and lit fires of sticks in the sitting room. So in the evenings we sat and listened to his talking.

For Gringoire was a conversationalist. Like most dynamic, overwhelming, and energetic poets, he had not the patience to listen to the remarks of his fellows or to answer. He would be silent most of the day. But toward evening, as like as not, he would suddenly suspend all his activities, and with very possibly a hair-sieve or a trowel in his hand, gesticulating too, he would begin to talk.

As a house party the Easter experiment was not a success for all of us. Gringoire had hardened himself in Flanders; the rest had not. But since, as a by-product of the experience, Madame Sélysette had consented to share and adorn his lot, Gringoire had his reward. And the writer secured these records of his monologues:

"I wonder," then, he asked on one of these evenings, "if my experience of landscape during the war has been that of many people." And without waiting he continued much as follows: "For I may say that before August, 1914, I lived more through my eyes than through any other sense, and in consequence certain corners of the earth had, singularly, the power to stir me." But from the moment when, on the 4th of August, 1914, the Germans crossed the Belgian frontier "near a place called Gemmenich," aspects of the earth no longer existed for him.

The earth existed, of course. Extending to immense distances of field-gray; dimly colored in singularly shaped masses, as if the colors on Mercator's projection had been nearly washed out by a wet brush. Stretching away, very flat, silenced, in suspense, the earth—*orbis terrarum veteribus notus*—seemed to await the oncoming legions, gray too, but with the shimmer of gold standards that should pour out from that little gap, "near a place called Gemmenich," and should obscure and put to shame all the green champaign lands of the world, as the green grass of meadows is put to shame and obscured by clay, water pouring through a gap in a dike. That was the earth.

There were no nooks, no little, sweet corners; there were no assured homes, countries, provinces, kingdoms, or races. All the earth held its breath and waited.

"And it is only today," my friend went on, "that I see again a little nook of the earth; it forms the tiniest of hidden valleys, with a little red stream that buries itself in the red earth beneath the tall green of the grass and the pink and purple haze of campions, the occasional gold of buttercups, the cream of meadowsweet. The plants in the garden wave in stiffness like a battalion on parade—the platoons of lettuce, the headquarters' staff, all sweet peas, and the color company, which is of scarlet runners. The little old cottage is under a cliff of rock, like a gingerbread house from a Grimm's fairy tale; the silver birches and the tall pines confront it; the sunlight lies warmer than you could imagine in the hollow, and a nightingale is running in and out of the bean-stalks. Yes, a nightingale of midsummer that has abandoned the deep woodland and runs through the garden, a princess turned housekeeper, because it has young to feed. Think of noticing that!"

During the four years that the consciousness of the war lasted, he had noticed only four landscapes and birds only once—to know that he was noticing them—for themselves. Of course, one has memories of aspects of the world—but of a world that was only a background for emotions.

Even, for instance, when one saw poor Albert, by some trick of mnemonics, from the lettering of the huge word "Estaminet" across the front of a battered house in the Place where, in the blinding sunlight, some Australian transport men were watering their mules, and one recognized it for a place one had visited twenty years before and had forgotten—even when one saw the remains of the garden where, twenty years before, we had waited whilst our lunch of omelette, cutlets, and salad was prepared, or even when one saw the immense placard with "Caution" erected in the center of the white rubbish and white rubble of the Place, or the desecrated statue of the Madonna, leaning in an abandoned attitude from the church tower—even then one was so preoccupied, so shut in on one's self, that these things were not objects that one looked at for themselves. They were merely landmarks. Divisional Headquarters, one had been told, was behind the N.E. corner of the Place, the notice-board was to the N.E. of one's self, therefore one must pass it to reach Divisional Headquarters. It was Headquarters one wanted, not the storing of the mind with observed aspects.

So Gringoire had four landscapes, which represent four moments in four years when, for very short intervals, the strain of the war lifted itself from the mind. They were, those intermissions of the spirit, exactly like gazing through rifts in a mist. Do you know what it is to be on a Welsh mountain side when a heavy mist comes on? Nothing remains. You are there by yourself. . . . And the only preoccupation you have with the solid, invisible world is the boulders over which you stumble and the tufts of herbage that you try to recognize as your path. Then suddenly the mist is riven perpendicularly, and for a moment you see a pallid, flat plain stretching to infinity beneath your feet and running palely to a sea horizon on a level with your eyes. There will be pale churches, pale fields, and on a ghostly channel the wraiths of scattered islands. Then it will be all gone.

It was just so with the three or four landscapes that my friend saw during the war. There was the day in 1915 when Kensington Gardens suddenly grew visible. There were Guardsmen turning in fours, with some Guardee form of drill that is not usual to the Infantry. There were motor transport wagons going cautiously down the Broad Walk—parts of the familiar train of the war. And then, suddenly, there were great motionless trees, heavy in their summer foliage, blue-gray, beneath a very high sky; there was the long, quiet part of the palace; the red brick, glowing in the sun, the shadows of the windows very precise and blue. And Gringoire thought that old, stiff marionettes, rather homely courtiers and royalties, might step out of the tall windows onto the lawns and, holding tasseled canes to their lips, bow, pirouette and make legs, till the long chestnut wigs brushed the stiff rosebushes. Not *very* gallant; not *very* royal. No Rois Soleils or Princesses Lointaines but a Court nevertheless, whispering mercilessly, intriguing, smiling, betraying, much as in Versailles, only a little more rustically, in front of the old, homely Dutch orangery.

Then the curtain closed again; the weight once more settled down. The trees again became the foreground and there was the feeling that Gringoire could never get away from—that they would be personally humiliated, shamed, abashed; as if they would wrathfully bow or avert their heads if ever field-gray troops passed down the Broad Walk, or the park keeper at the gates wore a Uhlan uniform! That was in the early days of the war—August, 1915, I think. The feeling that there might be an invasion was still, and was strong, in the air. There was no knowing, still, where the dam might give way and the mud-colored tide pour toward us. And somehow Gringoire figured it coming from the W. by S.W. from the direction of Kew and Fulham: high, gray, reaching from the legions on the ground to the gray airships towering on high—a solid, perpendicular wave of humiliation like the tidal wave of which one reads—of humiliation for the trees and the very grass.

"I wonder," Gringoire asked again that evening, "if other people had, like myself, that feeling that what one feared for was the land—not the people but the menaced earth with its familiar aspect. And I wonder why one had the feeling. I dare say it was just want of imagination: one couldn't perhaps figure the feelings of ruined, fleeing and martyred populations. And yet, when I had seen enough of those, the feeling did not alter. I remember that what struck me most in ruined Pont de Nieppe, by Armentières, was still the feeling of abashment that seemed to attach to furniture and wall-paper exposed to the sky—not the sufferings of the civilian population, who seemed to be jolly enough—or at any rate sufficiently nonchalant—with booths erected under ruined walls or in still whole cottages, selling fried fish to the tanneries. No! what struck me as infinitely pathetic was lace curtains: for there were innumerable lace curtains, that had shaded vanished windows, fluttering from all the unroofed walls in the glassless window-frames. They seemed to me to be more forlornly ashamed than any human beings I have ever seen. Only brute beasts ever approach that: old and weary horses, in nettle-grown fields; or dogs when they go away into bushes to die."

He went on to say that perhaps prisoners of war had it too. The Germans certainly seemed to. But he had, naturally, never seen any of our own people in that condition. They are represented to us as remaining erect and keeping most of their *esprit de corps*. That may be why, in August, 1915, it was difficult to think of the sufferings of our possibly invaded peoples but only of the humiliation of desecrated herbage and downlands.

"I don't know." And Gringoire meditated as if neither I nor Mme. Sélysette were in the room. "Perhaps I am lacking in human sympathy or have no particular cause to love my fellow men. But at any rate, at that moment, the feeling of dread that those gray-blue, motionless trees under the high sky might, under heavens more lowering, feel that final humiliation—that feeling was so strong that I remember it still as a pain. Nay, in the remembrance, I feel it so strongly that it is still a pain, like that of an old, deep cicatrized wound. For of course, it would have connoted that the broad and the small fields, copses, spinneys, streams, and heaths, stretching away to the quiet downs and the ultimate sea, would have felt that tread of mailed and alien heels." He remembered looking up to the sky in an agony. And then he became again interested in the Guards at drill beneath the trees—whose dressing never altered. Why did they turn in fours at the command "Left turn" when they were in column of route? Why didn't they form two deep? They were not doing sentry drill or any form of ceremonial that

the ordinary Infantry practice. The command was not: "In fours: left turn."

So the workaday frame of mind came back—and we carried on.

On hearing of the death of Lord Kitchener, he had another short moment. "I don't know," he wrote this in a letter, "whether the news had anything to do with it. I suppose it had. I will tell you. I was being motored to Dunmow Station, and when the car arrived at that little shanty, the stationmaster, whom I remember as quite an old man, came to the car-stop and just said: 'Lord Kitchener has been drowned.' He appeared quite expressionless, and I remember that both my companion and I laughed. I should say that I even laughed loudly. In those days and frames of mind, one reached, as it were, down to jokes obtaining only amongst rather simple people—and the joke underlying the idea of the drowning at sea of a man so supported by a whole land might have been quite ingenious in idea—like some joke of the reign of Queen Anne involving the raising of the sea above the dome of St. Paul's.

"But he succeeded in assuring us that Lord Kitchener had been drowned. 'The Field Marshal Commanding in Chief had been last seen on the nearly vertical deck, following a member of his staff.'—A good death for the man who had saved his land—and Europe.

"For speaking not as an expert speaks but still as a student of the temper of war and the *moral* of what in the Army is called 'the men' I have no hesitation in saying—and I don't apologize for saying here—that without the figure of Lord Kitchener the British Army would have remained negligible in numbers and would have taken a very small part in the war. And I suppose that, without the British Army, the war could hardly have been maintained to a successful conclusion."

At any rate, that was the way in which it appeared to Gringoire with a mind suddenly jumped into attending to this shocking fact from the designing of an aiming card for the Ross Rifle. For in those days it was his province to instruct in the use of that weapon nine hundred returned British Expeditionary Force, all time-serving men, and in consequence the toughest customers you could imagine. Indeed, it is difficult to imagine them.

They had every guile from a military point of view. They were adepts in absences, swingings of the lead, drunks, excuses, barrack-breakings, cheerful lies, and a desperate determination not to exhibit any glimmerings of intelligence, let alone any proficiency, in the use of any kind of weapon, let alone the Ross Rifle, which was a gimcrack concern at the best, with aperture sights and fittings like watch springs and innumerable ways of being put out of order. And you could put your nose in half and get yet another month in hospital as easy as winking by pulling back the bolt in any sort of rapid practice.

They lived—these desperadoes—in a tumble-down skating rink, and they exercised amongst the backyards and dust-bins of a great city, and such was the moral atmosphere of the shadowy and stifling vault in which this kind of khaki lived that when, at Easter, Gringoire proposed to bring in a priest to hear the confessions of the Roman Catholics with more convenience to them, the men sent three R.C. sergeants as a deputation to him. They said the rink was not a fitting place for a priest to see. And every one of them promised to walk three miles to confession and to perform all his Easter duties faithfully sooner than that a priest should see them as they lived.

A great cavern of a place that was, laid out in stalls

like a cattle market, where the officers labored intolerably filling up innumerable forms with an immense sense of pressure and of striving with tough men. A great sense of pressure. And he would walk up and down in front of the worst-dressed line that had ever been imagined—a fantastic line, for not one of the nine hundred professed to be able to stand straight on his legs—and Gringoire would exclaim gloomily and in alternation: "Thank God we've got a Navy" or: "Lord Kitchener says the war's going to last another three years; hang me if you blighters will wangle out of going back to France." Whereupon there would be groans down the line and a near-drunk man would whisper: "Good ol' Kitchener!"

It was out of that horseshoe-cavern of gloom in whose shafts of vaporous and disinfectant-colored lights moved these troublesome green-brown shapes that he had come for a very brief period of leave in a world that, again, included lawns, afternoon teas, standard roses, tall rooms, servants—not batmen, but with caps and aprons—pianolas—and no one, really, to clean one's belt; as well as discussions of that higher, wilder, finer strategy, in which, in one's capacity of a more or less professional student of tactics, one was so decidedly at a loss. Or perhaps it wasn't immediately from the cavern that he had come; perhaps it was from the Chelsea Course. But there, amongst the Guards, the Kitchener "note" rang truer and cleaner and more insistently. And at any rate, he was certainly going back to that atmosphere of strain and rush; into the desperate effort to teach thousands and thousands bayonet fighting, gas tactics, measures against venereal disease, sentry drill, dugout building, why they were going to fight, how to manufacture grenades out of jam-tins, the history of the regiment, and *esprit de corps*—and doing it all in desperate and bewildered haste, with the aid of sacks, hairpins, can-openers and Japanese rifles with the wrong sort of bayonets, under the auspices of an orderly room driven mad by endless reproofs from brigades, divisions, the War Office, the civilian police, Boards of Agriculture, county asylums, parents whose sons had enlisted too young, and young women who had married privates too often married already. . . . But coming from it or not, Gringoire was certainly going back to it and, in its desperate and fleeting atmosphere, the idea of Lord Kitchener was the one solid thing onto which our poor poet could catch.

So the stationmaster made it plain that Lord Kitchener was dead.

It was just one of those situations in which one thinks nothing—a change in the beat of the clock. Gringoire was sitting in the little open shed of a waiting-room, the only idea present in his mind being that his crossed legs were stuck stiffly out in front of him, their weight upon his left heel and both hands in his breeches pockets. Nothing whatever! Absolutely nothing! No war: an empty mind; a little open shed with benches; a hatchway in one plank wall where they served out tickets; a bit of platform; a high, brick signal-box with clocks or things ticking; a brick house, no doubt the stationmaster's. . . . The whole world, that was! And noiseless; and immobile. There was no France on the horizon; no English Channel. There was no awaiting of Zeppelins; there was no Right or Wrong.

And so the veil lifted for a second. The flat lands of Essex were there, stretching out; flat fields; undistinguished beneath a dull sky. He speculated on the crops; on the labor it took to the acre to put in those cabbages; on the winds that must sweep across the comparatively hedgeless spaces. The ground looked like a good clay. Plenty of heart in it, no doubt they would say in auctioneer's advertisements. But, on the whole, an unsmiling, foreign land. Not Kent or Sussex, but "the Sheeres." If one settled down here, one wouldn't know the postman, the tax collector, the old standers, the way they trimmed the hedge rows, the habits of the soil, or the course of the months, the brooks, the birds, the breed of sheep, the gossip, the local history—or the dead. A friendless, foreign country, the Essex Flats. . . .

And the southeastern saying came up into Gringoire's mind: "You see yon man: he cooms from Sussex. He sucked in silliness with his mother's milk and 's been silly ever since. But never you trust a man from the Sheeres!" . . . It is Kent and Sussex against the world—just as no doubt it is Essex and Hertford; and Somerset and Devon; the North and East Riding and Durham and Cumberland and Denbigh and Flint, against the world—and it's *never* safe to put long straw under potatoes when you dig them in, trusting to the wet to rot it. At that point Gringoire remembered in 1899 buying some special seed, called, I think, "1900," out of compliment to the coming century. He paid a big price; one hundred twenty shillings the hundredweight, I think. And he dunged them beautifully with rather long straw and artificial manure. But a long, long dry season came, and the Kentish land sloped to the south, and the straw dried, and the artificial manure never soaked down. He didn't get a quarter of a ton to the quarter acre.

On the other hand, under maize, if you can water heavily once or twice, long straw arranged in trenches, like pipes, is rather a good wheeze. It holds the water to the roots and maize will do with a topsoil like fire if the roots are cool. In 1899 Gringoire got some wonderful ears of sweet corn. And, toasted on the cob and buttered after toasting . . . !

He changed heels under the puttees and considered his garden in Kent. He was going to try growing potatoes from seeds—not from seed-potatoes, but from the little seeds that form in the green berries. And he was going to put a light, whitewashed paling behind the sweet corn, on the north—to reflect the rays of the sun. It should ripen the cob three weeks earlier! . . .

The Essex flats became again, slowly, visible land, planted with war-food. An airplane was going toward Bishop Stortford; the train was overdue because a unit was entraining up the line—once again every fact in the world was just a part, just a side light of the immense problem. Once again nothing existed just for itself. Trains were carriers of men and munitions. Stretched-out legs were encased in puttees, put in military boots; servant girls travelling with horn-handled black umbrellas and elastic boots were going to see their boys off at Waterloo; old farmers with white side whiskers were explaining why they had kept all six sons at home—in defiance of the gaze of Lord Kitchener that looked at them six times in that wee small station. And railway fares were going to be increased for civilians!

I have little doubt that what, at that moment and for that minute space of time, had set our poet intent on planting potatoes and seed corn—perfectly certain that he was going straight down into Kent to plant potatoes in rows and sweet corn in hills—was that his unconscious mind was certain that the war was done and over with that death in the North Sea. I do not mean to say that he thought it—or even that he was conscious that something inside thought it for him. His surface-mind thought certainly of Essex, of Kent and Sussex; the subconscious mind seemed to be aware that his puttees were badly put on, that he had mislaid his warrant in one of several pockets—he had a vague consciousness of South Wales, blue mountains, like Japanese clouds. But some deeper center still was probably appalled and benumbed and was saying:

"Now the war is finished and lost. Now, *'appry la gair finny'* as the Tommies say, *je vais planter mes choux comme un maître d'école.*" There seemed to be nothing left but to plant out a kitchen garden.

III

Blue of Swallows' Backs

WELL, by the evening of his next monologue, Gringoire had planted out his kitchen garden; the onions, the lettuces, the carrots, the kohl-rabi, the spinach were aligned; that battalion was parading in full strength. Moreover, in a bed from which he had just removed spinach and onions, there were twenty little potato plants, grown from little seeds: under a twenty-foot quick-set hedge, beautiful and close like a wall, the sweet corn was already up to the hips. The long straws, like pipes, ran in a trench under the corn hills; the deluge of water, warmed because it comes from a dip on which the sun blazes all day, washed the deep roots; the nightingale was running in and out of the beanstalks; the swallows were throwing themselves through the air; over the low brick the sun was setting on the longest day of the year, and, D.S.G., the war was over and done. No longer D.H.Q., Bn.H.Q., M.L.E.,

T.M.B.—but just D.S.G.! To God alone be the glory in the quiet garden evening.

"I will tell you a curious thing," said Gringoire in June, "but in gardens amongst woods, beside streams, there are so many curious things to tell of that I don't know where to begin! I am like a child with the largest coin it has ever possessed outside a hundred entrancing shops. I began talking the other day with the idea of describing four landscapes—the great guns from Portsmouth now remind me, though I have written of only two, of yet a fifth."

We—Gringoire and the writer—had been for a slow walk, round three sides of a patch of heath. A man, leaning over a white gate, with a thin, red face, a blue suit and some very bright regimental tie, just said: "The telegram's up in the post office. It's official!" And, speaking of it that evening in the warmth of the garden beside the hammock of Mme. Sélysette, Gringoire said:

"I assure you, on my honor, that the whole landscape, the commonplace, friendly landscape of elms, rather backward wheat, heather, gorse, and park-wall suddenly changed. It was as if the focus of the camera had suddenly clicked, readjusted itself—as if it grew—

though before one hadn't known it for anything but all that was possible of tranquillity, breadth, security, and peace—grew quieter, calmer, broader, more utterly secure and inviolable. English country!

"I don't know: there's nothing to it, really. A spray of dog-roses; a whitethroat dropping over the hedge; some gorse; the long, rolling land; the high skies and clouds above the downs. . . . Well, it is one stage more toward a forever of security, of that being forever inviolable that one prays may be its portion. A great stage forward."

For coming home and sitting behind irregular, all but too old lattice, giving onto a deep wall of verdure, we had heard suddenly the heavy guns through the voices of birds. . . . And Gringoire said later that, at the sound of those distant guns through the overwhelming orchestra of birds, he had seen distinctly, against the warm brick of the house-wall, a tin hat. . . . But many tin hats dim in the blue-gray light, and a lot of Scotch Jocks, their kilts covered with khaki aprons, and an immense long train with innumerable shapes dropping out of it, their cries muted by the twilight: the crunch of feet on the gravel, before the tin sheds of the station. That had been Railhead behind the Somme. And then suddenly you were conscious of the innumerable voices of birds singing the sun down. And then through them the uninterrupted heavy discourse of the great guns at a distance came over the little hills and darkling trees of that downland country. It continued. . . . Incessant, engrossed, almost as it were tranquil, almost like the bubbling of water in a pot, boiling up, dying down, going on and on, not penetrating but enveloping the cries of Tommy to Tommy or of footsteps to footsteps—and, rising through it, as if lances of sound were protruding upward through something soft and vaporous, the voices of thrushes. A great many thrushes: and the down getting whiter; and the "Fall In There's" and the men moving off . . .

So that he said he half wished the Portsmouth guns would stop—five-point nines; ninety-eight pounders; fifteen-inch guns—whatever they are. One doesn't want to hear them again, or again to feel them—dully on the air. Not at any rate in peace time.

The nightingale amongst the bean-stalks; the thrushes in the shaw on the opposite hillsides; the swallows throwing themselves through the air! He did not remember any nightingale during the war; but he remembered those thrushes of Rébimont-Méricourt on a date in July '16. And he remembered some swallows —an immense sea of the blue of swallows' backs. And he said that the Portsmouth guns of the 28/6/'19 sounding through the birds' voices from the hill opposite the Gingerbread Cottage brought it all back. Poets are like that and have these visions.

It sounds, of course, queer—but it was like that. Up on a hillside that was covered mostly with thistles there was an Artillery Observation Post which consisted of a Lombardy poplar—though one did not see how the gunners got up it. At any rate, there was a pile of dud Hun shells on the roadside bank at the foot of the tree and beneath the O.P. was a pretty rotten dugout with a corrugated iron roof. The Battalion Trench Mortar officer lived there. Below him he had a view of a battery of French 75's, of the chalky line of trenches; Martinpuich looked down on him, which wasn't overly comfortable, and the Ancre wound away—to No Man's Land. From time to time a field-gun wheel going along the road would catch its spokes in the corrugated iron of his roof—lift a corner and drop it again. I don't know why the Trench Mortar officer lived in that dugout, but a gunwheel lifted his roof and dropped it again whilst Gringoire was dozing in it. He thought the bottom of hell had dropped out. It was his worst shock of the war. I shouldn't wonder if it were not the worst shock any one ever had between the 4/8/'14 and the 28/6/'19. He mentioned it, he said, because it probably accounted for his immediately subsequent exultation; it was, I suppose, so good to be just alive after that.

At any rate, after the Trench Mortar officer had come in—Gringoire had been waiting to give him a message—downhill through the thistles, dusty in the hot sunlight, Gringoire went with immense, joyful strides. He said that he was extraordinarily fit in those days! And an innumerable company of swallows flew round him, waist high, just brushing the thistledown. "They were so near," Gringoire said, "that they brushed my hands, and they extended so far that I could see nothing else. It is one of the five things of the war that I really see, for it was like walking, buoyantly, in the pellucid sunlight, waist-high through a sea of unsurpassed and unsurpassable azure. I felt as if I were a Greek god. It was like a miracle.

"Now, I see swallows from below, their rust-stained breasts against high, blotted, gray clouds—and I wonder if they are thinking of the near rising mayfly. I remember thinking on the other occasion that there were a good many dead amongst the thistles and that I must be putting up a huge number of flies. But that, again, was the thought of my subconscious mind. On the surface I just felt myself to be a Greek god, immortal, young forever, forever buoyant, amongst the eddies of a dark blue and eternal sea."

The feeling lasted until he got to the mule-lines of somebody's First Line Transport, where he borrowed a terrible old brute of a horse, to take him to Divisional H.Q.

It would be interesting to know what that class of feeling comes from—possibly from some sort of atavistic throwback to days when the gods were nearer. You get them now and again in action—but not so often as you get the reverse type of feeling when you are engaged in agriculture. That is perhaps why farmers are so often passionately disagreeable and apparently unreasonable men. For there is nothing that so much resembles contact with, wrestling with, a personal devil as to awaken one morning and to find that a whole crop of seedlings has vanished before myriads of slugs. That happens. If you don't believe it, read White's

No Enemy

"Selborne." It is loss, ruin perhaps. It is like a death: a profound and unforeseen disaster. And your mind personifies the slug as intelligent, malignant, a being with a will for evil directed against you in person. I think that, whilst it lasts, it is the worst feeling in the world.

Drought is nearly as bad.

IV

The Kingdoms of the Earth

It was after Gringoire had speculated on slugs, without, you will observe, suggesting a remedy, that he continued:

"I have given you, so far, three of the landscapes that remain real to me—for the detraining in the dawn at Rébimont-Méricourt is not one of those that are just always in my mind. I have to remember back to—to be reminded of it. It was the sounds of Peace Guns pierced by the multitudinous voices of thrushes that brought back to me that first-heard, unintermittent thudding and throb of the engines of war through which, like spears, thrust the voices of innumerable birds. But, just, I suppose, because one's mind was preoccupied with the job of seeing that one's valise was all right, that the men had all their kit and equipment at least potentially there—and no doubt with the job of seeing to it that one's composure appeared absolute

—one recorded less of visible objects, so that fewer visible objects return, and they return less vividly."

He remembered—and he knew that he remembered, accurately and exactly—every detail of Kensington Gardens on that day of August, 1915; of the Essex Railway Station he said that he could tell you what advertisements were on the walls and how many people awaited the train as well as every word of the conversation he had had whilst driving to the station. And he remembered with an extreme clearness, as in the little paintings of Van Eyck on the Chasse de Ste. Ursule at Brûges, the swallows and the thistles of the ridge going down in the clear July weather behind Bécourt Wood in 1916. He had a job then, it is true—but not one calling for any immediate or complicated action. Besides, at that moment he had felt himself to be immune from danger and proof against death. So that those three landscapes became part of his immediate self.

"They will probably remain part of myself to the end of my life: my grandchildren will probably be tired of them and, when I am quite aged, so probably will guests and casual strangers." But—did you ever take a walking tour, or just a long walk and, in bed at the end of the day, perhaps in order to put yourself to sleep, did you ever try to remember every inch of the roads you had covered? Gringoire claimed that in that way he could remember a great many of the roads both of England and France of his boyhood when one walked or cycled a good deal for walking or cycling's sake. Corners of roads, bridges, highways climbing over the forehead of downs—the road out of Bridport, down into Winchester, from Minehead to Lynton; from Calais over the flats to Arras, from Arras to Beauvais; from Blois to Tours; from Amiens to Albert in 1892. . . . By shutting his eyes, or by looking at something blank, like a sheet of paper, or by not really looking at anything at all, he could, he said, evoke a panorama of any of those roads, or say from the North Foreland to Land's End. Perhaps he couldn't really, but he could have a pretty good try and get a lot right. "Well, in that way, I can evoke most of the roads 'round Albert, or Locre and the base of the Salient, or Bailleul, or Steenewerck, or Armentières; and plenty of other places of the Lines of Communication like Hazebrouck and Abbéville and St. Omer. But I daresay I should get some of it incorrect."

For instance, as to the detraining at Railhead in that dawn: he had distinctly the feeling that there was a woody, dark bank and a plantation of trees in which the thrushes sang, right up against the flat of the line. There wasn't really. He found later, on coming out of Corbie and there entraining to rejoin his battalion, that there were only high elms against flat, champaign country with a muddy stream. However, there was a high farm-building just behind the elms, so, no doubt, the effect on the inattentive eye was that. And the thrushes had certainly sung.

But he could evoke the rest of the road to the front line fairly well. On the right of the station, in the elms, was a brown Y.M.C.A. hut, where the officers got very greasy bread and rather black fried eggs and coffee. There were innumerable, old, dog's-eared magazines on the mess tables in amongst the breakfast utensils. Twenty or thirty numbers of the "English Review," like the dominoes, of a date when our writer used to own that periodical. It seemed an odd thing to see; an odd, queer thing to have owned. Near—too near—the hut were the men's latrines; a little further, the officers'. On the left, then, as the Draft passed, was the station. A very fat old gendarme was standing, well back on his heels, his legs wide apart; about him were four market women, with bundles, and baskets containing fowls. They were grouped around the gendarme like pullets around chanticleer, as he watched the sunrise. A lot of Royal Field Artillery horses and riders came over the dust into the station yard; a company of Jocks was waiting outside the office of the Railway Transport Officer. The ground was soft dust, so that the reinforcement might have been marching in sandals.

They continued their march parallel with the railway line, along a soft road, beside the little stream, between osier-bushes and elms—for about fifty yards. There were some stray mules belonging to a Kitchener's battalion, Wiltshires or Cheshires—Nineteenth Division anyhow. There didn't appear to be any drivers. There was a good deal of shouting; the Draft about-turned. The guide was taking them wrong. But who ever knew a guide take any one right anywhere? It was rather like a dream—not at all a bad dream—but, anyhow, a numbness.

Or no: really it was more like being in the hands of doctors, on the way to an operation. Probably the anaesthetic would be all right; it wouldn't hurt. At any rate, we had no volition; one's feet moved; one's haversack was a bit heavy—not very. One went on, one didn't know where.

In the same way you may remember the anteroom of your dentist. There is a big table in the center of the room; on the table some writing materials—and old periodicals, like the "English Reviews" amongst the solid Y.M.C.A. cups and plates. . . . But, on the one hand there is, solid and real, say, Mandeville Place: taxis drive about in it; the faces of the houses are of black-gray Portland cement, imitating granite. The street, then, is real: and the operating room will soon feel as real, even while one is waiting in the outer room. But the anteroom itself is a dream-landscape.

So it was with the Rébimont-Méricourt road.

When you come out of the station yard, on the right there is a high, white-walled, tile-roofed estaminet-farm. Australian First Line Transport men were watering their mules there, lounging on the steps with their tunics off. The road began to mount; on the left, on top of a high bank was an orchard. It reminded our poet of the nutwalk, on a high bank, belonging to a certain farm in Kent—at the bottom of Aldington Knoll, where the marsh begins. Mounting the slope, on the right, he came to a closed, empty, butcher's shop. A superior butcher's shop with grilles, green paint, gone of course dusty, marble slabs, and a gilded copper sign.

The road opened out suddenly. It was a dusty expanse between houses: in England it would have been a village green. There were house walls, windows, archways in the dusty white plaster, giving onto farmyards or stables. Two men were harnessing a black mare into a hooded, two-wheeled, dusty cart. Four black Percheron stallions were standing in a string in front of a long cottage. "They reminded me," Gringoire said, "of four black stallions I had seen, years before, outside the blacksmith's at Beaumont-le-Roger. In those days it had seemed to be odd that stallions could be left unattended in a village-street. But in 1916, I was used to that idea; what intrigued me, then, was that any civilian should have four stallions at his disposal. For they certainly were not French cavalry, or divisional or other transport."

The civilians seemed extraordinarily—not unreal—but, as it were, super-real! North French peasants, slow, ungainly, with heavy legs and feet. They were just the peasants one had always seen; hard, like granite—not comparatively soft and comparatively gray, like our own old peasants, who, when they look hard have the aspect not of wrinkled stone but of old, crannied, oak-tree boles. It was Sussex downland, that country—but like the people, harder, unsmiling.

To the left of the Place—if you can call a flat space of dust a Place—there was a narrow street, high, mud walls; archways, semi-circular topped, gray wooden doors. On one of these was nailed a large white placard: headquarters of the 4th Army Veterinary Corps. (I hope this is no longer a staff secret.) The reinforcement had to drop some men of the Draft they had brought out—men for the poor 38th Division that was to be wiped out in Mametz Wood—at some other sort of headquarters at the end of the street; that was why some of us penetrated it. Yes: it was very narrow and high-walled—more Wiltshire than Sussex! There must have been vegetation on the top of some of the mud-walls. Opposite the Farriers' H.Q. there was a little, thatched, sweet-shop sort of a place, and irises were growing on the thatch. I daresay they would not be there in peace time: you would say it was more Irish than French.

In the sweet-shop they sold dates, clay pipes, picture

postcards with English regimental badges, picture postcards with views of Albert and the toppling Madonna; silk-worked postcards of bright reds, whites, and bright blues, and postcards showing smiling ladies dusted with spangles. The women behind the low counter were very unreal: a motionless old witch with black eyes, a brown face, and dead white, parted hair; she stood, and only her eyes moved, and she appeared, not malignant, but grotesquely like a brown wooden image with moving eyes; an untidy dark girl, without even looking at us or at a perplexed Tommy who was pricing postcards, stood, her face sideways and repeated: "Ten . . . a penny: ten . . . a penny"—patiently, and as if from a great distance. She said: "Ten" very fast, then paused and added "a penny" slowly and as if with boredom. The Tommy grasped ten postcards and held out a penny, but she continued to say: "Ten . . . a penny, ten . . . a penny," without either movement or expression.

"So I could continue," our poet went on, "to recall this itinerary, for many pages and for many hours: past the farm on the right, with the great dung heap, past the pond overshadowed by crab-apples; past another crossroads on the right, where, at a tent, facing a great, dull-brick aggregation of ruins, rafters, and fallen chimneys, which was once a sugar factory—the timekeeper's office and the iron gates were still intact—we delivered up the remaining other Ranks of the Draft and went on, up the bare downland road, officers only, between the bearded wheat on the left and the immense field of thin oats to the right—upward to the Officers' Distributing Center; tents just put up that day, on a bare, downland field, very white and with the long down-grass still untramped in their interiors. . . .

"Yes, I could keep it up for many of your pages and for many hours," Gringoire said, "but I am not so much concerned to describe these landscapes, or to prove the quality of my memory, as to establish the psychological facts about the other four landscapes." He had just gone back into memory, without any particular effort—without indeed any effort at all, and the roads were there, like a string unwinding from a ball. His eyes must have been at work but not his registering brain. The mind was working otherwise.

"I have purposely omitted to mention," he said later, "that, all the way, on all the roads, proceeding generally with caution because of the worn *pavés,* but sometimes getting a swift run for a couple of hundred or so of yards, sometimes one at a time, sometimes four together, at times in as thick a stream as motor traffic in Piccadilly—the ambulances passed us, on the left."

That was a detail of the mind rather than of the eyes. Gringoire knew in 1919 that they were there, because he remembered that several of the officers had to count them for a time. But they appeared to be rather symbols than concrete objects. They stood for BLIGHTIES—going home! They were part of what made the skin of the forehead over the eyes feel always a little drawn, part of the preoccupation that, always, turned one's thoughts inward. I don't suppose it was fear—or perhaps that is how fear really manifests itself.

Here, then, is another landscape. It was up at the Officers' Distributing Center. Or perhaps it wasn't officially called that, though that was what it was. It may have been an Officers' Rest Camp—which it certainly was not. At any rate, there it was on an open, sloping downland field—seven new tents pitched, two more being pitched: cook-houses, wash-houses, latrines, batmen's quarters, and the rest of it, down to the incinerator, were all, also, in process of being erected.

The Senior Officer in charge of our party interviewed the Camp Commandant and the officers sprawled about on the bare hillside with the downland winds running over the grasses just as they do in Sussex on a cloudless day.

"I have always thought," Gringoire said, "ever since I was a small boy and used to ride on the downs behind Folkestone that the sun has a peculiar quality in the sky over downlands, as if chalk dust in the air whitened the rays. But that is probably nonsense." Anyhow, the field sloped downwards; there was a white cart—or plow—track; then up went a great shoulder of the downs in a field all purple sections. I suppose cultivation for the time ended in the huge field of thin oats between the camp and the destroyed sugar factory. There was a very old man in a short blue blouse, with immensely long bow-legs—doing something with a scythe. It didn't appear to be mowing.

The down rising over against them appeared—so unable is the eye to measure these swelling distances —quite a small affair. But, halfway up it, seeming to tight-rope along a white thread, with an extreme slowness in passing from point to point, went transport wagons, incredibly tiny. So it was an immense, august, shoulder. A near-mountain!

Gringoire said he could not just remember where the sun was: he ought to be able to work it out by the place and time. But I daresay it doesn't really matter. At any rate, over the shoulder of the down—not in the least like a moon or an astral body but illuminated by the sun—silver and French gray, very slowly, a great body began to rise. One hadn't much—one hadn't indeed any—sense of proportion. It seemed immense—and alive as mushrooms are alive. Then, induced as the eye was to look into the pellucid sky, there became visible a number—some one counted fourteen—of tiny, shining globes. They appeared to be globes, because there was a fresh wind blowing straight from them and they turned end on. So, but slowly and incessantly heaving, did the immense one close at hand; a spider's network of cordage went with its movements. Tiny and incredibly pretty, like films of gold dust floating in blue water and like peach blossom leaves—yes, incredibly pretty in the sunlight—airplanes were there. Because the—just as pretty—little mushrooms that existed suddenly in the sky, beside the sunlit dragonflies and peach blossoms, were pearly white, one officer said:

"Hun planes!"

The German shrapnel made black bursts. The officers were lounging in a group of six or seven. Another said: *"Their* sausages too . . . Out there! Fourteen!"

The slow ascent of our own sausage took the mind into the sky. A broad-faced, slow, brown, very sympathetic young officer—he had a rich voice, a slight stutter, and one eye that frequently winked—said:

"He showed Him the Kingdoms of the Earth." Then: "From a high place, you know, old dear," he explained, rather apologetically to Gringoire. "His career," Gringoire said, "was constantly interlaced with mine; in the stream that carried us along, we bobbed together—at Cardiff, in Rouen twice on June afternoons, and even after the Armistice, once in Coventry Street, and once in York. Yet, though we were quite intimate, he calling me 'Old Dear,' or 'Old Preserved Equanimity,' as my last Colonel nicknamed me, and though I called him 'Old Dear,' and later, as the fashion became, 'Old Bean,' I never knew his name. He would be there, in Orderly Room, in an officers' club armchair, at mess, dropping usually some single,

rather apposite, slightly literary remark—with just the trace of a stutter and always in an extraordinarily sympathetic voice—a deep, modest, affecting being. . . . I wish I knew who he was—but I suppose I never shall.

"He sh-showed Him the Kingdoms of th-the Earth," this officer said—and his voice just seemed homelike.

Some one else said, "Let's go up that mountain," in the true Welsh tone and accent, and several: "Yes, yes, let's. . . . Surely we'd see everything. . . . Surely to goodness, let's not miss it. . . ."

And they figured to themselves a glorious run down, and a glorious run up, the shoulder and then a great, flat gray view—of everything, and of all who mattered—of the Kingdoms of the Earth. But the usual voice—Conscience, Caution, Fear of Broad Views, maybe said: "We'd have to get leave. . . . The Camp Commandant, you know. . . . Eh, what, you fellows? . . ."

The Camp Commandant, a small, extraordinarily excited Highlander, voiceless with gas and gesticulating because of shell-shock—threw papers about, threw off his Glengarry cap, shrieked, wheezed, croaked. "I knew him quite well," Gringoire said, "and, since he once hauled me out of bed at four o'clock of a freezing morning because some sort of Scots Brigadier wanted some one to play 'Annie Laurie' and the 'Banks of Loch Lomond' to forty drunken Scots officers in another hut, I permit myself to talk of him as he was, capless, exacerbated, grasping a telephone and throwing things about."

He didn't know whether he could or could not give them leave to go up the brae; he didn't care if they went and drowned themselves. Couldn't they see he'd only been there forty meen-its and there were two hundred contradictory memoranda awaiting him? And oh to hell, and oh to hell. . . .

They loafed once more; they fell back into that eternal "waiting to report" that takes up 112/113ths of one's time during war. They contemplated and made remarks about the veering of the sausage.

It was then that Gringoire related a psychological anecdote that gives the note of this book. "I suppose it was my friend's sympathetic and suggestive voice that did it . . . for I suddenly began to see bits of a landscape that has pursued me ever since—until now here I sit in it. Not quite a landscape; a nook, rather; the full extent of the view about one hundred seventy yards by two hundred seventy—the closed up end of a valley; closed up by trees—willows, silver birches, oaks, and Scotch pines; deep, among banks; with a little stream, just a trickle, level with the grass of the bottom. You understand the idea—a sanctuary."

There were, in those days, you will remember, no more sanctuaries. All nooks of the world were threatened by the tide of blue-gray mud. We were out there to hold it back on the Somme. But could we?

So that was a little nook, sanctuary; where you said "Feignits" to destiny—with a gingerbread cottage out of Grimm. You were a Haensel, holding some Gretel's hand, tiptoeing, whispering, craning forward the neck. . . . A castle in Spain in fact, only that it was in a southern country—the English country.

"I ask to be believed in what I am now saying," Gringoire uttered the words slowly. "It is just the truth. If I wanted to tell fairy tales, I'd do better than this. Fairy tales to be all about the Earth shaking, and the wire, and the crumps, and the beef-tins. . . . You know. And that would be true too. Anyway this is. . . ."

He said that he didn't pretend that he was gay at that moment: calm, no doubt; contemplative certainly —and certainly gently ironic. So many officers were fussy about things—air pillows, hooch, mislaid movement cards, how to post picture-cards, where their battalions were, and so on. The place no doubt brought it out. It left a good deal to be desired. So that, if he could smile gently, he didn't pretend to have been without apprehensions. They hung vaguely at the back of the skull; they oppressed, a little, the breathing.

And yet—ever since he had been a tiny child—he had, he said, been so much a creature of dreads that this was, in a sense, much less than dreads to which he had been well accustomed. The dreads of original sin, of poverty, of bankruptcy, of incredible shyness, of insults, misunderstandings, of disease, of death, of succumbing to blackmailers, forgers, brain-troubles, punishments, undeserved ingratitudes, betrayals.—There was nothing, Gringoire said, that he hadn't dreaded in a sufficiently long life "which had been, mostly, a matter of one dread knocking out another." So that, on the whole, the dread of what lay over the hill was less than most and limited itself, pretty well, to how one's self would behave—except of course that one was damned afraid of being taken prisoner. Oh, damned afraid. . . .

Still it was on the whole such a relief to be out

of contact with one's civilian friends at home—for, as far as the Army was concerned, Gringoire said he never had one single moment's cause for bitterness, but just contentment and making allowances—it was on the whole such a relief that he was more contented than perturbed. Nevertheless, the strain was a long strain, even if it was impersonal, since it was a strain concerning itself with the English Country and not at all with one's regiment or one's self. One's regiment would go out, if things went wrong. It would go out, disappear, as sands disappear under great waves. One's self too, probably, or it wouldn't matter anyhow . . . But the contaminated fields, the ashamed elms—that was the long strain. And suddenly, at that point it came—the castle in the air; the simulacrum; the vision of the inviolable corner of the earth.

I don't mean to say that it came with great exactness at that time—but it came, no doubt as a progression from the train of thought in Dunmow Station. There, you may remember, Gringoire thought that he would have a garden in a southeastern county—and his thoughts had connoted that it would be a garden on a hillside that sloped to the south and that looked over a not very distant sea—a great view, showing on the horizon, during clear days, the coast of France; a view, as it were, from which one could see the Kingdoms of the Earth. "For there have," said Gringoire, "always been only two Kingdoms of the Earth that mattered for me—our own land for its country and France for her people, her arts, her point of view." Yes, undoubtedly it was to be a garden with a great view, and it should contain potatoes grown from seeds and sweet corn—also several rows of beans for which, whether for the flowers or the aligned stalks, Gringoire always had a great affection.

In Dunmow station it had been merely an intellectual idea: as who should say, "After the war, we will take a cottage in the country and grow things and have a great view. At any rate, we will have a rest." But, on the downside behind the Somme, it came differently. It came like one of these visions that one's eyes, when tired, will see just before one falls asleep. There was a rhomboid of deeper, brighter green, of a green that was really alive, beyond the gray-green of the field they were in. It existed in front of the purple of scabrous flowers on the great shoulder that masked the battlefield. It wavered, precisely as you will see the colored image cast on a sheet by a magic lantern, then slowly, it hardened and brightened, took shape as a recumbent oval, like eighteenth century vignettes. Gringoire said that it became perfectly definite—"The little view that I shall see at this moment if I raise my eyes. And it didn't connote any locality: it didn't, I mean, suggest itself as being in the vicinity of the Trossachs, of Tintern, of Matlock, of Dungeness. . . . It was just country—but perfectly definite, rather an untrimmed and a rather hidden spot without a hard road going to it . . . and with the feeling that many birds were lurking in bushes and watching me, as birds watch. You see the idea—sanctuary!"

"I don't mean to say," he went on, "that I wanted to get out of the battle of the Somme. I certainly didn't, either consciously, subconsciously, or with any plane of my mind. I will lay claim to so much militarism. But my subconscious mind was trying to assure itself that 'appry la gair finny' there would be a sanctuary where I would cross my second and my index fingers in the face of destiny and cry 'Feignits' as we used to do as children at Prisoner's Base. I daresay that has been the main desire of my life. I daresay it has been the main desire of the lives of all men since recorded time began. Unrecorded time too, no doubt. It was no doubt the basic desire that has given to the world in succeeding ages, the Kingdom of God, the Kingdom of Heaven, the Kingdom of Thule, the Cassiterides, the Garden of the Hesperides, the land of Cockaigne where hot mutton pies ran about in the street asking to be eaten—the peace of God which passes all understanding."

And you see it was mostly for the sake of the little threatened nooks of the earth that Gringoire found himself on that hillside. For, then, as on the 4/8/'14, when the Huns crossed the Belgian frontier, "near a place called Gemmenich," it was mainly the idea that a field-gray tide of mud was seeking to overwhelm the small, verdure-masked homes, the long, white, thatched farms of the world that forced Gringoire into political action. "All my life," as he put it, "I have been fighting German scholarships, German modes of learning, of instruction, of collectivism." But, before that date he hadn't much imagined—or imagined at all—that he would ever indulge in political polemics. He had always had a dreamy contempt for politics: one is an artist, one is a poet, one is a builder of castles in the air, one is a gentleman, a farrier, a grocer, a miller—what you will—but a politician! *"Ah, mais non.* That one should prostitute one's pen! . . ."

But the field-gray tide threatened—not only the Kingdoms of the Earth that mattered, but the little, sacred homes of artists, poets, gentry, farriers, grocers, millers—menaced then the subjects of one's pen, the objects of meditation of one's heart. So one wrote endless, interminable propaganda; until the brain reeled and the fingers stiffened.

Then the Germans killed Henri Gaudier and Teddy Jewell. Or prehaps it was only that Teddy Jewell went. Certainly he was killed sooner or later. "Such nice, good boys both—though I didn't know either of them well." So there had not seemed anything else to do. And indeed there was not anything else to do. . . .

Up there, on the hillside, that ran down to the battered sugar factory, he had the feeling that, if they could have had leave and have looked over the rim of that brown-purple slope, they would have seen the Huns, a white, tumultuous line, like advancing surf or like gnashing teeth. That was, of course, a feeling, not an intellectual idea. He knew that the German lines didn't look like that—though, indeed, at times they did, when our gunners really got onto them in a chalky country. Then it was rather like surf—the smoke of shells and chalk dust going up together in the sunlight. . . . Still . . .

And anyhow that was a moment of complete idleness—a moment of the completest idleness that those officers had known for many, many months. They were just there, with nothing to do. Nothing: nothing whatever. If they had been allowed to look over the hill-brow, that would have been something, but, with the Camp Commandant's refusal of leave, complete idleness settled down. In ten minutes, in an hour, perhaps; certainly before the passage of four or five hours, they would get the order to report that would take them beyond that hill past the battered sugar factory. . . .

Possibly that little vision of English country, coming then, was really a prayer, as if the depths of one's mind were murmuring: "Blessed Mary, ask your kind Son that we may have the peace of God that passes all understanding, one day, for a little while in a little nook, all green, with silver birches, and a trickle of a stream through a meadow, and the chimneys of a gingerbread cottage out of Grimm just peeping over the fruit trees." I suppose that is the burden of most prayers before battle. And of course that would mean that the Allies had won out and that the band would have played in the last war parade, with the white goat and its silver plaque between the horns, and sunlight, and even the Adjutant smiling—and all the Welsh dead appeased, and all the country nooks of the world assured sanctuaries, and every Englishman's house an inviolable castle, and every Frenchman free to potter off to his café in the cool of the evening. No doubt it was a prayer of the unconscious, tired mind.

"But even that isn't my fourth landscape," our poet-host went on, "since my fourth landscape took in very nearly the whole, if not quite the whole, of one of the Kingdoms of the Earth—and that the smallest that I ever hope to see." It dissociates itself sharply from the others in that the observing of it happened to be Gringoire's job of the moment. He had been sent up to Mont Vedaigne to mark down and be ready to point out to a number of senior officers all that immense prospect.

And the tip of Mt. Vedaigne formed, oddly enough, one of those little, commonplace, rustic, idyllic spots that, months before, had formed itself for his eyes behind the Somme. There, in a small enclosed space, shut in by trees that just grew up to the edge of the steep escarpments of the hill, was, precisely, a little, gingerbread cottage out of Grimm. In front of it was a small, flat garden—not an acre in extent; in the garden grew potatoes already yellowed; beanstalks were aligned, already yellowed too; and there may have been three or four rods of tobacco plants and as many of haricots, yellowing too, for the fringes of autumn were upon the land. On the southern side of the garden were some plum trees in a hedge. If you looked over the hedge you saw Bailleul, Armentières, away to queer, conical, gray mountains that were the slag-heaps near Béthune, and away, farther, toward the Somme itself.

On the northern side of the garden was a tall, dark plantation of birches and firs so that the gingerbread cottage—of white plaster, with little green shutters and a bright red roof of those S-shaped tiles that lock one into another, with a gutter painted bright green, like the shutters, and dependent from the gutter, right along the face of the cottage, bunches of haricot plants, hung up so that the white beans should dry in the rattling pods—the little cottage, then, had the air of being beneath a high, dark bank.

But it was only trees, so that, if you went between their trunks you saw another great view. A flat, almost incredibly immense, silver-gray plain ran right to the foot of the waving descent, below. There was an oval—poor Poperinghe—with an immense column of snow-white smoke, descending upon it from a great height, and then little plumes of smoke here and there—and then, away, away, pollarded flats, windmills, church towers—and a gray, menacing, incredibly distant skyline, illuminated under drifts of smoke. . . . One imagined that one was seeing into Germany!

I suppose Gringoire didn't really see so far.

On the east and the west, the views were cut into by "mountains"—the peaks of that little range of hills that formed practically all that remained of a Kingdom of the Earth—of the Low Countries! There was the Mont Noir with its windmill atop; the Mont Rouge with its windmill atop; the Scharpenberg, with its windmill, Mount Kemmel with its ruined tower, from high above which, in the pellucid autumn air, the sighting shells continuously let down their clouds like torsos of flawless, white marble.

Gringoire had emotions up there! And he had a long time to wait. You may not know it—but, if a senior officer tells you to await him at a given point at 10:00 A.M., you arrive at 9:45 whilst he saunters in at 11:00 A.M., 12:30 P.M., 2:00 P.M., or 4:30 P.M., according to his rank.

On this occasion, Gringoire was Acting Intelligence Officer, and, having to familiarize himself with a landscape in which his division had only just arrived, he came on the ground at 8:45 A.M., having left Locre at 7:00 A.M., riding round by way of Dranoutre to receive his final instructions from Headquarters. He did not think that at Divisional Headquarters his zeal was appreciated. A sleepy, but eminently indignant, General Staff Officer I or II, something elderly, in pajamas, made various insulting remarks about early rising. These, his eyesight improving as sleep departed, he modified somewhat, because he could not tell who the devil Gringoire was. (I may say that, two nights before, our poet had been court-martialed for being in unlawful possession of a Field Officer's Figure.) But the Major would not modify his statement that he had only been in bed half an hour. He stuck to it. I daresay, poor man, that he was telling the truth.

He was wearing khaki-silk pajamas with purple cords. Gringoire, on the other hand, stuck with equal firmness to the fact that he was deputizing for a brother officer who was sick—so sick that he had mislaid his orders. Orderly Room had sent them to him with a slip attached: *"Passed to you, please. For attention, immediate action and compliance."* They had had a copy of *that* slip in the Battalion Orderly Room—but no copy of the memo itself.

Apparently they hadn't at Divisional Headquarters either. It appears that the G.S.O. I or II who had issued the memo was sick too—had gone sick the night before and our elderly friend was deputizing for him. Of course, eventually, Gringoire got some sort of instructions from a drowsy, patronizing lance-corporal of the type that one usually finds around Divisional Headquarters, sleeping omnisciently under a table covered with typewriting machines in a Connaught hut. *He* knew that some one answering to the description of my friend was to meet some one on the top of Mont Vedaigne at 11:00 A.M. for the purpose of explaining the positions. It was some General, the lance-corporal couldn't remember the name—it was a name like Atkinson or Perry or McAlpine—an ordinary sort of name, the lance-corporal said contemptuously. He didn't know what sort of General he was. The General Staff Officer Number Two ought to have taken him 'round, but he had gone sick; so also had Gringoire's friend, who was a friend of G.S.O. II. So there he was.

("And," said Gringoire when he recounted this incident, "it occurs to me at this moment this was intended as a friendly attention on the part of somebody. Either my friend—who was highly connected in an Army sense—or, failing him, I—was to wangle a soft job out of the General. But all I thought about was how to get to the top of Mont Vedaigne, set my map, get my field telescope into position . . . Well, I am telling you what I thought about. . . .")

He was indeed so concentrated in mind on the top of Mont Vedaigne and the map and the compass and the telescope that he hadn't the faintest remembrance of the road thither from Dranoutre.[1] He said he could give you every object, estaminet, cottage, and Corps H.Q. from Locre to Dranoutre by the chaussée; or

[1] I am aware that D.H.Q. was not really at Dranoutre, which was a nice little place, built round a church square, rendered nasty by the Germans. But I call it Dranoutre out of reflex action caused by fear of the Censor—who once, at the end of 1918, struck out of one of my poems an allusion to the fact that I visited Cardiff early in 1915.

from Locre to Mont Rouge by second class road and field paths, Mont Rouge to Mont Noir, and Mont Vedaigne and so on. But of the road to Mont Vedaigne from Divisional Headquarters nothing remained—except that it was rather suburban, broad, white, and at that date, in good repair.

So he came to the top of the hill, passed the cottage without looking at it, between the potatoes and the tobacco and the tobacco and the haricots, looked over the southern edge, and saw a great stretch of country, looked over the northern edge, and saw a great, silver-gray plain, looked away to the east, and saw hills like camels' humps cutting still horizons; and the same on the west.

He was, you understand, in a desperate hurry. For each point of the compass, he "set" his map, finding a convenient, flat piece of ground on which to lay it. And he saw, without seeing, and memorized without associations—just names attaching to dark patches in a great plain. Over a particularly large fir tree was Armentières; over an oak, lower down the slope and to the right were the slag heaps and Béthune; further to the right still Bailleul; the flash of gilt above a steeple meant the ten block letters *Poperinghe;* an immensely distant series of dull purple cubes against a long silver gleam was, in printed capitals DUNKIRK. . . . You see, his mind was just working in the water-tight compartments of his immediate professional job. He wanted to make—and he did make by 11:00 A.M. —four cards, like the range cards one makes for musketry: a central point where one stood, and arrows, running out like rays from that center, toward Ypres, in capitals or Wytschaete in block letters. He wanted the general to be able to stand on each point, look down on the card, follow the direction of the arrow, and identify the place. I don't know whether any other Intelligence Officer ever thought of that. Anyhow, he got it done by 11:00 A.M.

It was pleasant, the feeling when he had made his last fair copy. He went to each of the points of the compass, to make sure that he had registered positions truly. Returning from the west to the east, he noticed an immense plane, appearing in the firmament above Bailleul. She was escorted by eight or nine relatively little monoplanes—Bristol scouts, I should say. But, at that date, the poor bloody Infantry were not brought much in contact with the air force. So that, apart from their spectacular, picturesque, or dangerous aspects, they hardly came within the scope of Gringoire's professional attentions. "Airmen," he said, "were brilliant beings, who treated us with contempt and carried off the affections of our young women. Otherwise they lived in the air whilst we plodded amongst mud and barbed wire. Professionally, they rivaled the Cavalry; obtained information for the Artillery—but, as for co-operating with us, we were below their notice." So that the great, beautiful machine—which was, I believe, the first Handley Page to reach France in safety—passed overhead without Gringoire's thinking of more than that it was beautiful.

But his time for consideration of the beautiful had not yet come. It being then eleven and his work as a man from Cook's being accomplished, he had time to think of breakfast.

He had noticed that a cottage existed behind the potatoes, the haricots, and the tobacco. His conscious mind had dismissed it, since it had obviously no topographical value as an object of interest for a General, name unknown. His subconscious mind—that of an Infantry Officer—had also dismissed it—as just a cottage; too frail to be of much use for cover, even against rifle fire. For you are to understand that whilst his surface mind was entirely and devotedly given to his immediate job, his secondary mind had certainly taken note of the values of Mont Vedaigne, the garden, the hedges, the copsewood, the timber, and the slopes; considering them as cover, as sites for trenches and noticing the fields of fire, the dead ground, the trees that would be dangerous in falling about if the place were shelled, the underwood that might be useful, supposing the Artillery had failed to knock it to bits or set fire to it—it was very dry still—before the Enemy Infantry tried to rush the position. All these little thoughts had flitted, like shadows, to be registered somewhere.—For our poet learned that, when, ten minutes later, he went over the ground again, for the definite purpose of considering it with conscious, infantry-eye, he had already noted and stored somewhere in the gray matter of his brain most of the details of dead ground, field of fire and sites for trenches, too . . . and a good deal of the detail as to timber, underwood, and the like.

That, however, was only after he had had some breakfast. For a little old Belgian woman with a pepper and salt face and a husband who wore a black cap with a shining leather eye shade, came out of the green door of the cottage, just as the lady does in a weatherhouse. To Gringoire's request in Flemish for coffee, *"Hebt gii Kafe to verkoopen?"* she answered nothing, disappearing backwards behind the green door, which shut as if automatically. She was there again, however, in less than a minute, with a plate of ham, a bowl of coffee, and four bits of their gingerbread!

The significance of this did not occur to our subsequent inhabitant of a gingerbread dwelling. He only noticed that it did not go so very well—nor yet so very badly—with the ham. He ate both, anyhow, in a hurry. It was a keen air up there. He secured some more ham and another cup of coffee and, with that in his hand, proceeded to the clearing in the east from which the best view of the Salient was obtainable.

It was then that the Infantry Officer's hitherto subconscious, professional mind rose to the surface and became the conscious one. In the four hours that he had waited in that frame of mind, he had noticed, of course, an infinite number of details—a great number of airplanes coming from the direction of Dunkirk; huge columns of smoke rising from far back in German-held Belgium, behind Brûges. A great number of signs of war in that clear, gray, sunlit space, in which every pollard willow appeared to be visible and like a candle flame burning in a windless air! Gringoire was looking through a telescope, of course. But I will trouble the reader only with two apparitions of those that he collected: they were apparently unconnected, since they took place, the one at Poperinghe, the other in front of Wytschaete. But very likely they had a grim connection.

Whilst he was topographically employed, our Infantry Officer had noticed Poperinghe as a blue-gray smudge, in shape like an oval lozenge seen in perspective. From it rose several church towers—bulbous, Low-Country edifices. Now, whilst he was resting his eyes from the telescope, he saw, suddenly unfolding in the air above the towers, two great white swans. They extended laterally, dazzling, very slow. Then a trunk descended from each of them. After a time they resembled, exactly, immense torsos of Hercules, headless and armless statues, as solid-looking as brilliant white marble, new from the quarry. The Tommies called them Statue Shells.

And then he noticed that there were statue shells over the observation post on Kemmel Hill. With his telescope, also, he began to see that shells were bursting on Poperinghe. I don't know why, but he took them to be gas shells, bracketing.

He rested his eyes again and looked at the gap between Mont Noir and Mont Kemmel. It was a symmetrical bit of landscape seen over what is called technically a saddle between two hills. Over the very center of the lowest part of the dip, Gringoire said, there appeared to be a whitish gray tooth stump, decayed, with one end-fragment rather high.[1] Extending, like a long string, above this, on rising ground, there was a brown rope—five miles, perhaps beyond the decayed tooth. Little white balls existed on the brown line, the landscape was pale yellow—as it might be the gold of corn fields. The red roofs of a village that he knew to be Wytschaete were brilliant and quiet in the sun—but, on the brown line beneath that ridge the little white balls went on coming into existence—one every half second. One to the right at the extreme end of the line; one on the extreme left; one in the middle; one between the extreme left and the center. Beautiful work. Have you ever seen a village cobbler nailing a

[1] This would be the remains of the Cathedral and the Cloth Hall at Ypres.

sole? It goes so quickly that you hardly see the hammer. But a small brass nail is there—and another and another—a line of brass nails on the smooth leather. Well, they went like that, along the brown line—the little white balls! Beautiful! Beautiful work. "My mind," Gringoire said, "was filled with joy and my soul exulted in the clear, still, autumn sunshine, looking over that tiny Kingdom of the Earth.

"I said to myself: 'Hurray! The guns are giving them hell. Some one's ducking over there.' " Because, of course, the brown line was the Hun trenches on the Wytschaete ridge, and the little white balls were our shells, falling with an exact precision. They must have knocked the trenches pretty considerably already for the disturbed earth to show at all at that distance.

At that moment—it was just gone three—a man in khaki made Gringoire jump by appearing at his elbow. He said that the General who had ordered Gringoire to report there at 1:00 P.M. was detained. Would he have some lunch and report again at the same spot at five?

And, after that, it was just emotions. The landscape became landscape, with great shafts of light and shadows of clouds; the little white cottage with the green shutters, a little nook that should be inviolable; the haricots interesting as things that one might plant in a Kentish garden that sloped to the sea. The range of hills was no longer a strategical point or a tactical position. It was all that remained of one of the Kingdoms of the Earth; one could hardly look at the gray plains with the pollard willows marching like aligned candle flames toward the horizon—one avoided looking at it, because it was Lost Territory, held down, oppressed, as if it were ashamed. Poperinghe grew to appear pitiful, a little town where wretched civilians were being butchered by gas shells for the love of God. So the poet's mind worked, at leisure, on personal matters, as neither the mind of Intelligence, or Infantry, Officer need work.

"My mind," the poet reports, "was indeed so much at leisure in that long two hours that I even wrote in my Field Pocket Book a preface to a volume whose proofs had that morning reached me. In that I recorded my emotions of the moment and there, in a printed volume, they stand. It does not alter their value as a record of emotions that I subsequently learned that the statue shells over Poperinghe were not gas shells but had been discharged so as to give the

German Heavies the range, or that, upon reflection, it appears to me that the Germans were hardly shelling the town so profusely just for the love of God. They must either have heard that we had a considerable body of troops in the town, or else they were trying to stop, by that retaliation, our own artillery's heavy shelling of their Wytschaete-Messines positions."

But at any rate, there the emotions came, crowding and irrepressible. So that, just before, in the dusk, at seven o'clock, Gringoire saw the bright red flash of a brass hat's band in among dark fir trees, he noticed, with a sudden lift in the side, a light silver streak, behind the map of Dunkirk. It was the sea.

"And suddenly," he said, "there came upon me an intense longing to be beyond that sea." It was a longing not for any humanity—but just for the green country, the mists, the secure nook at the end of a little valley, the small cottage whose chimneys just showed over the fruit trees—for the feelings and the circumstances of a sanctuary in which one could cross one's second over one's index finger and in the face of destiny cry: "Feignits."

It was, however, necessary to stand to attention, and through the falling twilight to point out hardly visible towns to a nearly invisible Senior Officer. And immediately the mind went back to its original position: Dunkirk and Ypres became circles named in large capitals; Wytschaete and Kemmel were again in block lettering. One said: "The sea is just visible in that direction," and it was just a geographical fact.

V

Intermezzo

The day after peace was declared seemed to your compiler an excellent moment on which to remonstrate with our poet as to one of his characteristic locutions. The day was fine, cloudless, soft and still; some gardening operation of Gringoire's had consummately succeeded. I forget what it was. I fancy some long-studied contrivance of his had checkmated the slugs in his strawberry beds. At any rate we sat in the long grass by the hedge under the damson trees at the bottom of the garden over a great blue china bowl of strawberries which Gringoire characteristically insisted on moistening with red wine and sugar. He said that taken that way they were less gross than with cream and I am bound to say that Mme. Sélysette shared his views with which I could never agree.

In any case, it was with singular mildness that, lying on his side in the long grass, Gringoire answered my remonstrances.

"Why, no," he said, "I do not see why any one should object to the use of the term 'Hun' as applied to such members of the late Enemy nations as were not in arms against us. I do not care much about the matter and, if the word offends you, I will try, when I think about it, not to use it. But the fact is that I certainly never thought about it much at any time. It is a convenient phrase to use about what was evil in the people we were fighting against. I should not now—and I never did—call Brahms anything but a German composer nor should I ever think of calling Holbein a Hun painter or the Brothers Grimm of the fairy-tales, Boches. So that the word is a convenient one for differentiations. In effect for me the German musicians, painters, poets, working men, postmen and soldiers in the trenches or at their Headquarters were never Huns. I assert that categorically and I think it was true of the majority of my comrades—except that the majority of my comrades had never heard of Bach or Beethoven or Heine. But it was true that the majority of my comrades with whom I discussed the subject at all seriously, though they may have used the word you dislike, never—when talking seriously—used it as a term of hatred. Humanity will inevitably use a monosyllable in place of two sounds if it can get the chance and so will I.

"But I don't think many people in the trenches actually, and except at odd moments, ever felt active hatred against the men in the opposite lines or even those who militarily directed their operations. When they are not called on to be trustworthy or imaginative or to show human sympathy, men in the bulk are beasts fairly decent and fairly reasonable. We hated and objurgatively called "Huns," to the furthest extent of its Hunnish hideousness, not the poor bloody footsloggers who were immediately before us. No, the word applied itself to the professors, the prosaists, the publicists, the politicians who had sent those poor blighters to prevent our going home. For if you think of it, it was a topsy-turvy arrangement. They wanted to send us home and we wanted desperately to go; yet they pushed towards our home and we away from ours. . . .

"I am not much set to talk to you about the trenches or even about fighting. The point that I want to put into the spotlight of your mind is mostly the fact that if we do not economize in food there will be another war. Unlike you, my dear Compi, in that I regard the past with much greater equanimity. You remember that, when we were both writing propaganda I used to shock you by the mildness of mine. It will be long before I forget your emotions when I wrote an article suggesting that, instead of atrocity-mongering we were sufficiently advanced along the road of civilization to write—at least of the German troops—as 'the gallant enemy.'

"Today our positions have changed and you are shocked because I style certain of those who belong to the late Enemy nation by an epithet that you wish to forget having employed. The point is that I stand where I did whereas you have reacted against what now appear to have been your extravagances. My propaganda, as you remember, was almost entirely a matter of economics and of culture. I simply pointed out that the war was in effect a hunger war: Prussia being mostly composed of immense sand wastes—the Lüneburger Heide; of impenetrable forest—the Teutoberger Wald; and of the vast stretch of swamps where Hindenburg massacred the Russians on their own border. That being the condition of Prussia, the country would not produce enough food for the population which was also a population of the most prolific breeders in the world. I also pointed out—and I think I was almost the only person to do so—that the Enemy Empire instead of being the flourishing concern that she had bluffed the world into considering her was actually on the point of bankruptcy and losing trade after trade to foreign nations. That again was merely a matter of food. Germany had flourished on low wages and subsidies to manufacturers; but as food-prices rose the world over the wages of the German laborer had to go up so that, even with subsidies, the German manufacturer could no longer compete with us, the Italians, the French or even the South Americans. That Germany invaded Belgium may or may not have been the *triste nécessité* that her statesmen alleged it to be, but that the war, regarded as a food war was in very truth a sad necessity for her you may be perfectly convinced. Prussia was starving, her population was increasing by leaps and bounds, emigration had been forbidden by the government. . . .

"Well, I do not propose to hate a starving population that seeks for bread, but I do propose to dislike and go on disliking the professors and publicists who preached that the only way to obtain bread was by invading Belgium and I do not think that the epithet you object to is any too strong. And indeed, if you use it merely to designate what was hateful in the late Enemy nation and if you employ the word 'German' for everything that was and is *'gemütlich'* for those who since yesterday have been our friends, you will be doing them a service by emphasizing what they have of the lovable in their compositions. Still . . . I do not much care about that.

"I do not believe that there will ever be another war if you put it only on the baser ground that the great financiers who alone can make or stop wars got hideously frightened by the last one. And in addition to that you can consider the educative effect of the Armageddon that finished yesterday. It will take a good many decades before any human soul will again regard war as a means of enrichment and a good many centuries before any Great Power will again imagine that to have an aspect of bestriding the world in jackboots and with the saber rattling is of advantage to itself. It is a better world on the 29th of June, 1919, than it was on August the 3rd, 1914. Bluff has got its deathblow.

"Yes, the world is better and sweeter. We simple people are freed of an enormous incubus; we can sit still for a space and think, which we never could before in the history of the world. But of this I am certain—that what danger there is to the world and us is a food danger. I do not believe there will ever be another war: I believe our sufferings, great as they were, achieved that and were a small price to pay for that benefit. So, if you want to you may bless even the Huns as having been the occasion of our learning that lesson. But if there were ever another war it would be a war purely and simply for food.

"The food-producing soil of the earth is already occupied; the population of our small planet increases by leaps and bounds. I know enough about agriculture—and scientific agriculture at that—to know that the pretensions of scientists to increase the production of food by improved culture is weary nonsense when set against the consideration of the increase in the numbers of mankind. The most honest scientist that I know refused to reveal a method of increasing the yield of wheat sixfold on a given plot of ground because he satisfied himself that to do so in one year rendered that plot of ground absolutely barren for ten years and the milder improvements of agricultural processes that are evolved each year do not suffice to provide enough food for the extra mouths that each year are produced by Prussia alone.

"So that the position might seem pretty gloomy, but I remain an optimist, at least in the matter of war for if, as I think will prove the fact, there will be no war till the world is driven to it by starvation, then the coming of war may be so long delayed that, all races of the world being at last at much the same pitch of education, it will be obvious to them all that war is no way to increase the production of food. I heard, not a Hun, but a Swedish professor say the other day that it was terribly irksome and irritating to his countrymen to consider that, whilst they were overpopulated and cramped up on an infertile soil, down in the fertile south there was the nearly empty and extraordinarily fertile land known as France. And how, he asked, could France with her selfish inhabitants who regulated their birth-rate—or who at any rate selfishly refused to beget children to the limit of their capacity—how could France expect to enjoy immunity from invasion by the healthy, voracious and formidable Northern races who openheartedly and with splendid generosity begot children, to use his own phrase, by the bushel?

"I did not, as you might imagine, because of my obvious Gallophilism try to bite off that blond beast's head because what he said was, as to its premises, true enough. France *is* sparsely populated and wealthy, Sweden *is* overcrowded and infertile. But the remedy for that is not to be found in invasion: the solution is there, waiting. France which is the only country civilized enough not to overpopulate herself is at present the only country in the world that welcomes immigration and facilitates to the extreme the naturalization of immigrants.

"The Swede went on grumbling that it was very hard that his compatriots must expatriate themselves in order to enjoy those *Südfrüchte*—fruits of the South. He said that his fellow countrymen loved their graynesses and contracted terrible melancholias beneath Southern suns. . . . So that the only thing was raiding!

"I did not continue the discussion for I did not wish at the moment to hate a Swede. But that in essence shows the root of the matter. Wars will cease when nations and Northern Professors are sufficiently civilized to let nations be relatively nomadic and permit races to flow freely from inclement, overpopulated and infertile regions into those that are sparsely populated and fertile and not hyper-philoprogenitive.

"You may put it that hatred and overpopulation go hand in hand, their destination being war, and you would not be far wrong. For it is not the hatreds begotten after wars are declared that matter; those die natural if slow deaths as soon as the not very protracted activities of warfare are over and done with, so that it is only the hatreds that precede wars that need much concern us."

He went on to say that pre-war hatreds, apart from those inculcated by hungers of one sort or another, arose largely from differences of manners. We used to hate the French because they ate frogs and were elegant; they hated us because we said "goddam" and ruled the seas. But manners tend to approximate the world over with the extension of means of intercourse. They jazz in Cambodia as in Coney Island today and tomorrow they will speak American in the county of Clackmannan even as in Monte Carlo.

That Gringoire applauded. It was, he said, all to the good to have a dance that all could dance. Before the war the vigorous poor went to dogfights, cockfights, badgerfights: now they jazzed. It was a progress towards sweetness and light, part of what we had paid for with our sufferings. . . .

It was at this point that your Compiler became a little impatient. He had come to get war-reminiscences from a practising poet—but these colloquies resolved themselves into a continual struggle of wills, Gringoire persisting in dilating on the future as seen by the practising agriculturist and gastronome. And indeed, scenting that your Compiler was essaying to head him off from the topic on which his mind was fixed, he now went off upon a tirade about intensive horticulture and French cooking that lasted until dusk was well falling on his garden. And Madame Sélysette, raising her delicate eyebrows, intimated sufficiently plainly that, if we did not want a storm he had better not be interrupted.

The main points of his harangue were to the effect that humanity would be saved—if it was to be saved—by good cooking, intensive horti-, as opposed to agriculture. And of course by abstract thinking and the arts. And the avoidance of waste. Above all by the avoidance of waste.

To the pretensions of the scientific agriculturist he opposed the claims of hand-culture, to those of the popular restaurant upholder those of the meticulous chef. Hand culture whether of beasts, grain or vegetables gave a better product, the careful and intelligent cook gave you more appetizing food. The more appetizing your food the better you digested it and the less you needed to support you. He said—but that was on the question of waste—that in a French residence of the size of the Gingerbread Cottage you would not find enough waste to fatten a chicken with; in his own establishment, do all that he could, aided by Mme. Sélysette, they had waste enough to half fatten a pig. . . .

In short the world was to be saved by observing the precepts of the recipe for mutton chops with which your Compiler opened this little work. But all this seemed so apart from anything that his readers could be supposed to want from a book devoted to the war-reminiscences of a poet that your Compiler had long ceased to use his pencil and notebook before Gringoire had finished his sunset harangue, so that, having no notes of the arguments we may well, as to that matter, here inscribe the words: *"cetera desunt."*

But, having eased his mind, Gringoire became good-natured, and, becoming good-natured he was awake to the outer world. So he observed that Mme. Sélysette and your servant had for a long time made neither objections to nor comments on the stuff of his harangues. His voice had gone on sounding alone save for the churnings of an early night-jar that sat upon the gatepost giving onto the rushy meadow. And suddenly he stopped and laughed maliciously.

"Poor old Compi," he said, "how extraordinarily this isn't what you come for. But the stuff of war-reminiscences concerns itself almost as much with what war has made of a man as with the pictures that he saw. Still you are not the sort of person to see that and, in a minute I will reward your patience with a landscape that, though it has nothing to do with our main theme, may make a nice *bonne bouche* for your little book.

"But I do want to get in—just for the sake of pointing it out to the world—that the late hostilities, whilst they profoundly modified the manners of the world did, in their very nature, hold up to the world a moral that will be of infinite value as soon as the world is in any condition at all to notice it. That is to say it did teach us what a hell—what a hell!—of a lot we can do without.

"Take my dear Sélysette there, with her upbringing amongst the suns and luxuries of the *haute bourgeoisie* of the South. Do you suppose that if, before the 3rd of August, 1914 you had proposed to her to unite her destinies to the least pecunious of poets and take up her residence in a rat-ridden cottage beneath the usually lugubrious but at all times capricious skies of this septentrional land—do you suppose that, if you had then made that proposal she would not have crushed you to the earth with the mere weight of her scorn? Or take me. Would you, knowing me as you did in earlier but, I assure you, not half such happy days—would you have imagined me spending what till then, but not till now, were certainly my happiest hours in a bare hillside in a tent with absolutely no furnishings but an officer's camp-bed? I had been used to a good deal of luxury, but there for the first time I found peace though the German artillery was actually at that moment shelling that spot and I was for the first time under fire.

"That is one of the things that I remember most vividly, not because it was the first time I was under fire but because I felt that for the first time I had cut absolutely and finally loose from all the bedevilments of life at home—from the malices as from the luxuries. Afterwards, unused as I was to the artillery mind or its methods, I wondered a little that they should be so persistently shelling *us* and that they should find us with such accuracy.

"I was sitting on the side of my camp-bed talking to an extremely intoxicated and disheveled elderly officer who was nevertheless a man of no ordinary talent. That is to say that his harangues about everything under the sun were interspersed with a great number of classical quotations of singular aptness and he had also made several inventions that eventually proved very useful during the war and that saved him from a courtmartial for drunkenness. I was—as was so frequently my case—in charge of him and, although he was in no position to get away, I did not care to go into a dugout as did all my brother officers who had hitherto been in the tent with us. And indeed the fact was that that fellow's boozy conversation interested me. . . .

"The German shells came in groups of three, doing obviously what we infantry were taught to call bracketing. That is to say that the first three shells whined wearily overhead and caused a considerable rumpus in our mule lines that were perhaps a hundred yards behind us, and immediately afterwards a rocket or something like it let itself down from the heavens. A few minutes later three more shells fell short of us by perhaps another hundred yards down the hill. There was an obvious German plane overhead and it was in the late evening, nearly dark in the tent and quite dusk in the calm light outside.

"My elderly friend wagged his head sagely. He explained that the Germans were trying to find with their shells something that that plane thought it had seen—probably the great park of German captured guns that were just above us. They would fire three sets of three shells each. Then our heavy artillery would open on them as a gentle hint to them to be quiet and not disturb the serenity of the Sabbath evening. They might take the hint or they might not. If they did not a regular duel between the heavies would begin, and the earth would shake for miles 'round.

"But, in any case, he said—and his air of wisdom convinced me as if Solomon were returned to earth and judging artillery—that we should be left in peace very shortly. And at that moment the next batch of three shells arrived right on us. That is to say that one landed right in the middle of the captured German guns, one in the fortunately soft ground of a spring about thirty yards from our tent and one in the middle of the canteen tent that was just next to ours; so that immediately after the immense concussions innumerable crepitations sounded from the canvas above us, the clay, gravel and mud falling from where it had been precipitated into the skies. And a tin of sardines, coming through the tent-flap, landed as if miraculously in my lap. . . .

"But that old fellow went on nodding his head as if he had been a Chinese bronze and exclaiming: 'Don't get up! Don't get up! That will be the last of it!'

"And, sure enough it was. Immediately afterwards Bloody Mary and two of her lady friends let off, enormous and august, breaking the quiet night. And I suppose the Germans were not in the mood for any extended artillery duel. They had probably satisfied themselves that the German guns parked above us were duds of sorts. The plane must have observed them earlier in the evening and had signaled their presence with rockets. . . .

"But the point that I want to make is that no matter how simple your surroundings or limited your income you can find happiness as long as you are also surrounded by a set of men with incomes similarly exiguous who are contented with their surroundings. The German shells were an added discomfort which I don't adduce as part of my argument—as if it should be raining or indulging in any other eccentricity of weather that one cannot control.

"Anyhow, I have been happier in a tent or a hut or even in a dugout than ever I was in a night-club before the war or in the sort of a hotel they call a Grand Palace, and I would rather inhabit a Connaught hut furnished exclusively with biscuit or beef boxes and sluice myself with cold water in the open on a freezing morning than dwell among Park Lane millionaires and take my ease in a hummums. And, if I can do that, all humanity can. I am no exception, and it is in that way that salvation lies and the extinction of wars.

"Indeed, I can assure you that one of the most troubled moments of the war happened when, as I will later tell you, I was sent for to Paris by the French Government and by them lodged in circumstances of extreme luxury in a Palace on the Avenue de l'Opéra. For apart from the botherments of being asked to do propaganda that I did not want to do and the obvious hostility of the French officers with whom I mixed and momentary shortness of cash I had, as again I will tell you later, the extreme botherment of being introduced suddenly into the sequelæ of a very violent divorce case. A British cavalry officer had used a week's leave in going to Switzerland and carrying off his little daughter who had been taken there by his wife on her elopement with a "fiddler-fellow." And, as I sat in the vestibule of the Hotel Splendide et de l'Orient the little girl, whom I like to think of as Maisie—that Maisie of Henry James' book—came and without a word of any introduction, settled herself in my lap and went to sleep. She was bothered because she could not find the tram to Heaven. Because they said her mother had gone to Heaven.

"You would say that such things do not happen in war. But they *do*. . . . And the distracted cavalry officer having left me in charge of his sleeping daughter went on some business that he had at the Embassy. But before he went he pointed to the swinging doors of the hotel giving into the streets and told me that at any moment he expected his wife to rush in and use a revolver. . . . And I was due at the French Foreign Office for an interview upon which my future in the service and the world might turn.

"Eventually my publisher came in and I dropped the sleeping Maisie into his lap. He was to have accompanied me to the Ministry but I thought he would be more useful to me there, so I left him. . . . But I assure you I was much more frightened of the idea of Maisie's mother whom I pictured as a sort of infuriated Carmen than ever I was of any German shells. It was she, with her revolver, who typified for me real hatred—the woman robbed of her child. Whereas, as for the only man that I actually and consciously shot at and who actually and consciously shot at me, I never felt the ghost of an emotion of hatred. I was aware of imbecilely grinning when he missed me—as if it were any other sport—and of saying to myself: 'That's the sort of dud *you* are,' when I—and repeatedly—missed him. And I believe I felt regret when some one else killed him. At any rate I am glad that I cannot remember his face. . . .

"But Maisie's mother would have been a different affair. *She* would have been filled with hatred—as I don't believe that other fellow was—and I should have been paralyzed. . . . Why, even at this moment I can almost feel her revolver bullet entering my stomach. And I should have deserved it. One should not connive at the carrying off of a woman's child however righteous the case of the husband. It is perhaps a worse crime than crossing the Belgian frontier, 'near a place called Gemmenich.'

"To die thus would be to die in a bad cause. And I daresay that why I don't believe that any great hatred existed between the actual combatants in the late war —and why I don't, when I think about it, stigmatize the fellows who lately stood armed over against us as 'Huns'—is simply that we thought we had a good cause and that we knew that they also thought that they had a good cause. They thought that we endangered their homes as much as we thought that they endangered ours.

"So that I simply do not believe in atrocities. The worst fellow that I ever came across on our own side—an enormous Scot whose principal conversation was taken up with the topic of the prisoners he had murdered—I have seen become lachrymosely sentimental over a German prisoner who was in a lamentable state of funk at having to undergo a medical examination. That Scot almost blubbered over that Hun in his efforts to assure him that the doctor would not operate on him against his will. . . .

"No, I don't believe in atrocities. Or at the most I half believe in one. It is asserted—the Huns asserted it themselves but I found it difficult to believe—that they filmed the *Lusitania* whilst she was sinking. That I find atrocious. It is bad enough with premeditation—and the presence of a film operator would seem to prove premeditation—it is bad enough, then, with premeditation to sink a ship loaded with sleeping women and children. But if we concede that those responsible believed—as they may have done—that the *Lusitania* carried munitions of war even that may be nearly condoned. But that you should take a cinema machine to represent, for the gloating of others, the ruin and disappearance of a tall ship—that seems to me the most horrible of crimes. *Spurlos* is in itself a suspect word, a part of the vocabulary of ruthlessness that lost the Huns—not the fighting men—the war. But the real lives of men are enshrined in their products. To kill a poet is a small thing; to destroy his work is an irremediable offense. . . . And the most beautiful of all the handiwork of men is the tall ship. It is horrible to see houses go down in ruin under artillery fire; it is horrible to see fields mutilated and rendered unfertile or merely humiliated by the heels of alien conquerors. But to see a ship, its heart broken, its bows appealing to the heavens, slowly and mutely disappear. That is horrible. The sea shudders a little where it was. Only a little. But still the sea shudders.

"Obviously in wars you must sink ships. And I suppose you may make records of the sinking of ships if it be done pitifully. But, in a spirit of gloating, to represent for the purpose of affrighting others or making yet others gloat in turn—to make cold-bloodedly the record of the disappearance of the proudest ship in the world, that seems to me the most horrible of . . . *Schrecklichkeiten*. . . . But perhaps they never did it. Perhaps they only said that they did. That would be a queer way to make yourself popular!

"But there was a landscape that I wanted to tell you about.

"A little in front of Kemmel Hill we had some trenches—horrible trenches because of the nature of the ground. You could not dig down three feet because you came to water so the parapets were merely sandbags and the parados nothing at all. They must have been responsible for the loss of more lives than any other position of the whole war. In addition, when it rained, all the flood-water of the uplands poured down into them. Why I have seen them filled with cigarette packets washed down from our always luckless canteen—after the great storm in September '16.

"Well, it was just before then that we had been set to occupy those lines. If they had been retired a hundred and fifty yards they would have been on the slope of the hill and dry and safe. But the staff—or some bellicose individual on the staff—in spite of every representation preferred to lose a third of my battalion, let alone thirds of all the other battalions that occupied them, rather than to lose the little bit of prestige that it would have meant, by a retirement. Of a hundred and fifty yards! Think of that!

"Anyhow, there we came down in the early hours of a September moonlight—into a world of beautiful, bluish and misty calm. There were those calms in the line when the vengeful activities of seven or so million men had exhausted themselves and their imaginations had just gone to sleep. You would have long periods of quiet. They would be broken by sudden bursts of machine gun fire and flares of Verey lights when some bemused sentry had taken it into his head that half a dozen corpses in No Man's Land were stealing upon him. One's nerves did that in quiet, moonlit moments. You would look at a corpse, or some sacking, or some sandbags until you could swear they were creeping upon you. Then in a crisis, 'bang' would go your hipe, and off would go the machine guns, and up would flare the Verey lights. The guns too might come in and some poor devil or another lose his life. But as a rule silence would settle down again for another long period. . . . I wrote a poem about that, in French. But I never heard of any one having read it."

It was at that moment that your Compiler burst in with the words:

"Oh, it begins with: 'I should like to imagine a moonlight in which there will be no machine guns.' I heard my friend Mrs. Carmody recite it only yesterday. Recite, not read it!"

Gringoire grunted slightly.

"The point was that it was most beautiful moonlight, before a blue, silent mountain with mists dim all up its flanks. And the other point was that we, as you may remember, were a flying division. We were used for reinforcing threatened points or for resting overtired troops. And, facing us, the Germans had similar divisions that they called '*Sturmtruppen.*' The curious thing was that either their Intelligence was so good or ours was so good that whenever we were moved up or down the line we found the same regiments in front of us so that when we were on the Somme we fought the Second Brandenburgers, and when we moved up to the Salient there we found the Second Brandenburgers in front of us and after we had been in front of Armentières for a little, there sure enough were the famous Second Brandenburgers. The Cockchafers, they were nicknamed. After that they began to desert to us a good deal and they were replaced by the Würtembergers whom we used to consider better fellows, I don't know why, for we never, in the nature of the case, consorted much with either.

"On the occasion of that moonlight night the Brandenburgers had got in before us and displayed a natural curiosity to know who we were when we got in. The German—or rather the Hun—method of trying to unmask the identity of opponents was to sing national anthems. I use the word 'Hun' here because only a

Delbrueck or a Bethmann-Hollweg—a professor or a politician—would have thought of anything so ingeniously imbecile. For naturally we did not fall in with that little idea. . . . The idea, by the bye, was that if we were Scots and they sang 'Scots Wha Hae' or Irish and they sang 'The Wearin' of the Green,' or for us 'Hen Wlad Wy Nadhau' we should, in a burst of patriotic emotion either cheer or join in the chorus. We didn't. I remember that once when, no doubt suspecting who we were, they had tried singing "Ap Jenkin," which is our quickstep, our men replied by singing the imperial Chorus from the 'Mikado' as if to show that we were Japanese. That irritated them so much that they pounded our trench for an hour and a half with everything they could think of.

"On this occasion they tried everything from 'Rule Britannia' to 'Australia, Australia,' and elicited no reply. And then they suddenly touched off an immense gramophone that sang, through the still moonlight . . . the 'Hymn of Hate.' And in English!

"It was curious and eerie to hear that passionless machine let off those dire words devoted solely to ourselves, for they never evolved anything like it for the

French or the Belgians or the Italians or Annamites or Cochin Chinese or Brazilians. Now it screamed and brayed:

> "Hate of the head and hate of the hand,
> Hate of the breed and hate of the land
> ENGLAND
> Hate of the standing and hate of the lying,
> Hate of the living and hate of the dying
> ENGLAND . . . ENGLAND"

("And as a detail I may add that they had to get an English renegade—for there was one!—to make that translation.)

"I am bound to say that it made one shiver a little. There were the moonlight, and the mists, and the lights of poor Wytschaete far away on the ridge. And those words creeping towards us. It is perhaps more disagreeable to think of being prayed to death than of being shelled. One shivered.

"And when it fell silent one wondered if anything in the war or in the world could surpass it for drama. But one was wrong. You don't know the Welsh. They are the incomparable singers of four-part music in the open air.

"I remember, years ago, being on the side of a Welsh mountain on a Saturday evening at sunset and far below a Welsh miners' beanfeast was going along a thread of a road in char-à-bancs. And as each filled car passed there came up the sounds of four-part songs, incredibly sweet and incredibly mournful in the falling darkness. They are a conquered people, the Welsh, and their music is the music of a conquered people.

"But on that occasion the Germans had delivered themselves into their hands in the endless struggle between Saxon and Celt. For suddenly a single voice in 'B' Company began to sing with extraordinary clearness:

> 'Maxwelton braes are bonnie
> When earlie fa's the dew. . . .'

"And extraordinarily, before the singer had come to 'there that Annie Laurie,' the whole of 'B' Company was crooning out the other parts of the song. Beneath the moon. And then the whole Battalion, along a front of a mile. Crooning, you know, rather softly, not shouting. . . .

> "And for Bonnie Annie Laurie . . ."

"It was a good answer.

"They were forbidden of course to sing Welsh songs,

or it might have been 'Land of My Fathers' or the 'Men of Harlech.' As it was, it was better.

"But there was not much hatred about that. And you will observe that even the Huns had had to get a machine to do their hating."

VI

Just Country

It is one of the burdens of advancing age—as it is one of the penalties of having been unreasonably prolific—that one is always haunted by a vague dread of repeating one's self. One's mind, presumably, progresses, one touches and retouches one's ideas; hammers at the wording; seeks after a final clarity of expression. It is all one that one may have already printed the matter of the theme; the mind continues to work at the phraseology until one, finally, isn't certain that one has or hasn't sought the crystallization of the press. So it happens that I cannot be certain whether I have or haven't printed already what I am about to write. It can't, however, in the nature of things, have been more than a shortish article; so that if I have to apologize to any readers, the apology can't be for any great fault.

I fancy that what I then tried to put on paper was suggested by a letter that our poet wrote, having another moment of leisure, at about the time of his long wait for the General on Mont Vedaigne. I wrote an article, and certainly it was suggested by a passage in one of Gringoire's letters to a friend, at some one's request, for the journal called the N–. And that journal called the N– refused to print the article because it was too militarist. I don't myself see where the militarism can have come into the expression of what was pure speculation of a psychological kind—but censors, whether military or anti-military, are queer people, and I presume that their main job, as it presents itself to their minds, is the suppression of ideas. . . . The more I think about it now, the more the thought hardens and takes shape; some one—connected with the propaganda-ministry—*did* ask me to write an article for the N– and the N– did refuse to print it. I daresay the journal had quarreled with the department in between whiles.

Anyhow, the psychological speculation wasn't very profound, or, as far as I can see, very likely to render conscription a permanent institution in these islands. Stated in its baldest terms, it merely amounted to saying that when you are very busy with a job, you do not much notice what is going on around you. You don't, of course.

And, in the end, that is the basic idea that underlies these records of four landscapes. Gringoire was simply trying to state—or rather to illustrate—the fact that, during the whole of the period from the 4/8/'14 till the date when the German plenipotentiaries appended, in the Salle des Glaces, their signatures to the peace treaty, he only four times achieved a sufficient aloofness of mind to notice the landscape that surrounded him.

"I don't mean to say," our poet summed the matter up, "that I didn't have 'leaves,' but, for one cause and another, my leaves weren't ever pensive or leisurely. One was snatched into the civilian frame of mind—but into a civilian frame of mind that was always preoccupied with 'The War'—that was, indeed, in odd ways, far more preoccupied with the war than were one's self and one's friends. Thus I remember that, on the occasion of my first return from France, being in a Tommy's tunic, before I had arrived at the barrier of Viltona, I was stopped by an Assistant Provost Marshal and told that if I didn't immediately procure leather gloves, another sort of hat, a collar, a tie, and get rid of my divisional mark, I should be put under arrest and returned to my battalion. In the booking office, I found a telephone—which cost thruppence, instead of tuppence—and when I remonstrated with a lady who three times gave me a wrong number, I was told to remember that there was a war going on. When, there being no one in my own house, I tried to go by omnibus to my club for lunch, I being in mufti and a little lame, a lady conductor put her hand on my chest, exclaimed: 'There's a war on,' and very neatly threw me back into the road.

"When I got to my club, a civilian of an eminently moral appearance was lunching at my table. He addressed me condescendingly—as no doubt one would address a Tommy if one were a civilian at a club. I had the feeling that he was about to offer me a glass of beer—therefore I hurriedly began to talk of peace. I wanted, you see, to consider peace and to avoid at once the offer of a free drink and the remembrance of my comrades who were still in danger of their lives. I admit that my words were inconsiderate, for I simply said:

" 'Won't there be a high old fortnight's drunk after that day!'

"My table companion drew himself up, pursed dry lips, and as it were hissed:

" 'I think we have taken very good steps to prevent that.'

"He wouldn't, you see, let me forget my poor comrades who were still in the trenches. I do not remember what I said then; but only his attitude as with his napkin very white and crumpled in his hand, he removed to another table. Straight from that club I went to the house of an Eminent Reformer who told me that he would rather we lost the war than that the Cavalry should have a hand in winning it.[1] He couldn't know that it wasn't so very long since I had seen the empty saddles of the Deccan Horse, as, all intermingled with the men of some battalion of Gordons, they returned from an adventure in No Man's Land, during the 1916 Battle of the Somme. So I went

[1] Our friend is here venting a little of the bile that, as will be seen, at times obscures his outlook on life and makes him, elsewhere, appear ungenerous to the civilian population that so loyally did its bit. The train of thought of his friend the Eminent Reformer would seem to be as follows: (a) this is a war for liberty; (b) the Cavalry are officered mainly by the hereditary aristocracy; (c) if the hereditary aristocracy wins out in the war, liberty will suffer; (d) it would be preferable to lose the war. This seems logical. Our poet, however, refuses to see matters in this light. He says that he has never since spoken to that Eminent Reformer, who was once the closest of his friends—and that he never will again. This is lamentable. But is there not a tag beginning *"Irritabile genus . . . ?*

and had tea with a lady who gave me three milk biscuits from a silver tray and said: 'This *must* be a change from your hardships over there!'

"They *wouldn't,* you see, let me forget the poor dear fellows who were still in the trenches. So I passed the night in a Y.M.C.A. hut, discussing Mametz Wood of the 14/7/'16 with an officer of the 38th Division."

That, of course, was rather a special day, Gringoire said—though it was nothing out of the common. Given his age, former career, and surroundings, he couldn't be expected to come in for any huge amount of the salutary dissipation or the healing hospitality which did so much to *remonter* the *moral* of the troops. Moving mostly amongst the Intelligentsia, he came a good deal in contact with Conscientious Objectors who abused him to his face for militarism or with literary civilians of military age who, after calling at his house, returned to their own and wrote him anonymous but easily recognizable letters, the purport of which was that he had never heard a shot fired and that the only gas he had ever smelled had been emitted by himself. To balance them, he received a number of letters from the German population of London, threatening to murder him on account of his propagandist writings, whilst one of the most frequent preoccupations of his military career arose from the anonymous letters addressed to the War Office, to his various Colonels, and to the officers and other ranks of his regiment by a professional man whom he had once employed and who, after he lost that particular job, found that his conscience as a patriot demanded that he should continuously but unsuccessfully denounce our poet as a German spy.

That is all in the day's journey. *Homo homini lupus.* But it is not to be wondered at that in his periods of leisure Gringoire was not in a position to pay what he would have called a hell of a lot of attention to landscapes—or, in the alternative, that the essential call, of the land, of the war, was not the humanity that England contained—but just the country.

Possibly the idea of country—just country—postulates the idea of human companionship—but that is not the same thing as humanity.

"When I was a boy," as Gringoire put it, "every hedge and every turn of a white, long road, concealed a possible Princesse Lointaine." In those days one walked on and on—from the North Foreland to the Land's End; from Kensington to Winchelsea, from Minehead, by Porlock and Brendon, to Water's Meet. Or one cycled from Calais to Beauvais, by way of Arras; from Paris to Tours and along the Loire, somehow ending at Houlgate and Caen. Or one went in a slow fiacre from Amiens to Albert, ostensibly to see the new brick and mosaic cathedral, with the Madonna atop. But, no doubt, whether one went to Mevagissy or Mentone; Port Scathow, Pontardulais, Château Gaillard, or Curt-yr-Ala, one was really chasing the Only Possible She.

"Nowadays one sits in a green field—any green field—and longs for nothing more than just a little bit of loyalty. One longs, that is to say, that one may at last find the *hominem bonæ voluntatis* that one has chased all one's life. Possibly one desires that, resting one's eyes in the green of the grass as—do you remember, old Dai Bach?—according to the maxims of Color-Sergeant Davis of Caerphilly, we used to rest our eyes from the targets by looking into the trampled green blades, one longs to discover some formula that shall make us ourselves forever loyal to some ideal or other. . . .

"Or perhaps it is just rest that one wants. Anyhow, one wants the country that is just country—not heaths, moors, crags, forests, passes, named rivers, or famous views. No—just fields, just dead ground, or fields of clover that have never heard and will never hear the crepitation of machine guns; hedgerows unwired and not too trim, with a spray or so of bramble just moving in a wind from which one is sheltered. That, until the other day, one so seldom saw in France—or in England either, for that matter."

"I remember," Gringoire said in one of his anecdotes, "being in a wood—behind Tenby, I think, or near Manorbier or Pembroke, in 1915. It was very warm, and that part of Wales is a sleepy country. I had bicycled ahead of troops afoot to inspect some sort of position that, the day before, with my over-meticulousness, I had already spent hours in surveying, when I might have been listening to Pierrots. At any rate, I had three-quarters of an hour of entire leisure.

"The sun beat down; I was just inside the edge of a wood. A little marsh—a reëntrant—ran right in under the trees. There was a mill where the insignificant valley opened out; a little dam where the road mounted an opposite slope. And then, though I had sketched, in a military sense, every clump of rushes, every contour, every bridge, every railway cutting and bit of embankment, many times—suddenly this place of greenery assumed—that too!—the aspect of being just country.

"A little Welsh sheep poked its horns through the hedge and looked at me; a wren crept through a tangle of old thorns at my elbow, a nuthatch pursued a curious and intricate course amongst the netted, coarse fibers of ivy on a wild cherry-trunk. I lay still in the dappled sunlight and thought nothing, except that it was good to stretch out one's limbs, recumbent. Because the level, green ground in front of me was so grown with rushes, I began to try to remember what were the provisions of the Field Drain Act of the middle of last century. Surely the farmer could obtain from the State, on easy terms, a loan with which to defray the expense of soil-pipes and labor for the draining of that land. And I began to think about the queer, stodgy, Victorian mind; and about Albert the Good, and the Crystal Palace, which in those days was known as the Temple of Peace; and I remembered John Brown and John Morley and John Bright and John Stuart Mill and Mr. Ruskin and the rest of them, and mahogany chairs with horsehair seats and Argand lamps and the smoke and steam that used to fill the underground at Gower Street station. And in those days I had a 13-hand New Forest pony and a very old governess car and went to market on a Tuesday. . . .

"And then, quite suddenly, I felt that, for thousands and thousands of miles, on the green fields and in the woodlands, stretching away under the high skies, in the August sunlight, millions, millions, millions of my fellow men were moving—like tumultuous mites in a cheese, training and training, as we there were training—all across a broad world to where the sun was setting and to where the sun was rising—training to live a little, short space of time in an immense long ribbon of territory, where, for a mile or so the earth was scarred, macerated, beaten to a pulp, and burnt by the sun till it was all dust. . . . The thought grew, became an immense feeling, became an obsession. Then Major Ward, on a bay with a white forehead, appeared on the little bridge that carried the waters of the marsh beneath the road. The others were coming!"

VII

Playing the Game

As WILL appear in my last chapter Gringoire insists that I shall include in this volume a specimen of his prose written under fire. As that was written in French your compiler flatly refused to insert it in the body of his book so that, since Gringoire flatly refused to let the book appear at all unless it *was* included, it will be found elsewhere than in the body and what follows is his translation. I confess to regretting its inclusion for although I myself and a great number of my friends including even Mrs. Carmody who is the wife of the headmaster at the ancient grammar-school, a foundation of Edward VI's in the XVI century at which I have the honor to teach English Literature —although I and my friends consider him a very great poet, if not the greatest poet in the world at the moment, poet's prose is well known to be too florid for the real connoisseur of prose. And what follows is actually his own translation and Gringoire himself has asserted many times both in private and in public that he is entirely unable to translate his own prose. It does however present a picture of the poet under fire—a matter as to which he here refuses to say anything elsewhere under the plea that to talk about actual fighting disturbs his subsequent sleep with nightmares and also that he intends to treat of fighting subsequently himself when both the public bitterness and his own emotions shall have diminished. This decision I regret. For who in ten years' time will be found to take an interest in the late struggle whereas enshrined here in the amber of my own prose the record of his emotions might well interest people who have such memories still vivid within them. I may say that I myself, a journalist of considerable prewar practice, never went to the front though I served during the whole war in the depot of Gringoire's regiment.

Here then is Gringoire's prose, the original French of which he says was written at Pont de Nieppe during September 1916 after his visit to the French Ministry which he will describe in my next chapter.

A CRICKET MATCH

BEING A LETTER WRITTEN FROM THE LINES OF SUPPORT IN FLANDERS TO CAPTAIN UN TEL IN PARIS.

Mon cher monsieur, camarade et confrère (Gringoire's addressee was also a poet soldier):

Behind Bécourt Wood, on a July evening, whilst the shells of the Germans were passing overhead, we were playing cricket. The heavy shells went over, seeming to cry in their passage the word "We; e; eary"; then, changing their minds farther on they exclaimed peremptorily: "Whack!" But when one plays cricket one forgets the Hun orchestra; one does not even hear the shells that pass overhead. We were running about; we were cursing the butterfingered fool who dropped a catch; we even argued about points of play, because the rules of such cricket as one plays with a tennis-ball, two axe-helves for bats and bully-beef-cases for wicket—those rules are apt to be elastically interpreted. But no match England v. Australia at Lords' itself was ever so full of incident nor so moving as our game behind Bécourt Wood. The turf was of clay, baked porcelain-hard by the almost tropical sun;

for grass there was only an expanse of immense thistles; boundaries and spectators at once were provided by the transport mules in their lines. But we cheered, we gesticulated, we rushed about, we disputed, we roared . . . we—British infantry officers who are said to be phlegmatic, cold and taciturn.

I present the considerations that follow in the form of a letter to you, my dear Un Tel, though I would rather have written a balanced, careful and long-thought-out essay. But I cannot chisel at my prose today. "Ker wooley woo," as our Tommies say, "say la gair!" I have passed twenty-five years of my life in trying to find new cadences; in chasing assonances out of my prose, with an enraged meticulousness that might have been that of Uncle Flaubert himself. But today I only write letters—long, diffuse, and in banal phrases. The other demands too much time, too much peace of mind. . . . Ah, and too much luck!

Well, then, we were playing cricket when I saw passing close to us a French officer of my acquaintance—an officer of one of those admirable batteries of seventy-fives whose voices were so comforting to hear by day and so let us sleep at night. For when they spoke in their level and interrupted roll, hour on hour, at a few furlongs behind our backs—when *they* spoke, no Hun barked. And they were at that time aligned wheel to wheel from Albert to Verdun. The man was a gray-blue Colossus, his eyes brown and somber, his mustache heavy and dark. He stayed there, planted on his legs and his heavy stick, like some instrument of war, three-legged, silent and of steel. And when I left the game and went to talk to him he said to me in English:

"I find that a little shocking. *Very* shocking!"

And he continued to look at the players who went on gesticulating and running about amongst the giant thistles and the dangerous legs of the mules. I exclaimed vehemently:

"Au nom du bon Dieu, pourquoi?"

He did not take his eyes from the players and reflected for a long time before answering. And I, getting impatient, went on talking vehemently and even indulged in gesticulations. I said in French:

"Nous sortons des tranchées. . . . We are only just out of the trenches." This game made you fit, *remettait le moral,* made you forget the war. . . . What do I know of what I said? He kept on reflecting and I talking French. At last he said:

"I find"—he was still talking English—"that this war should be a religion. On coming out of the trenches one should sit . . . and reflect. Perhaps one should even pray a little. . . ."

And I . . . I went on arguing with him for a long time without his answering anything but:

"I find it, all the same."

And suddenly I burst out laughing. The situation seemed suddenly allegorical. And if you think of it, my dear friend, you will see how it was that I laughed. It was because it was he, the descendant of Cyrano de Bergerac, who spoke English in the monosyllables of a stage Lord Kitchener whilst I, the representative of so many officers and gentlemen who for many centuries have never found anything more to say than "O . . . ah!"—I who ought to have been wearing an eyeglass and blond whiskers was engaged in waving my arms and shouting a French that was rendered almost incoherent by emotion. And all my comrades—officers as well as other ranks—went on shouting, gesticulating, running about, cursing and laughing like children of Tarascon in the French South.

* * *

And in truth the change is astonishing and a little moving. We have always had the idea—even the French have had the idea—that the French people, and above all the French soldiers and French officers, were gay, debonnair, loquacious, pawky—"Swordsmen and tricksters without remorse or scruples," as Cyrano sings.

Well, the other day I went on service from Steenewerck to Paris—a journey which lasted seventeen hours. And during the whole of those seventeen hours although there were always French officers in my railway carriage or standing in the corridors of the train, the journey was the most silent of my whole life. No one talked. But no one! There were colonels, commandants, captains, marine officers, gunner officers. And I cannot believe that my presence was responsible for this taciturnity. It is true that in every suitable spot in the train were inscribed the words: "Be silent; be on your guard"—and the fact that enemy ears might be listening to you. But it was impossible that *all* those gentlemen attributed such ears to me. I was wearing the uniform of my sovereign. And they none of them addressed the others.

No, certainly the voyage lacked incident. I will tell

you the incidents there were: from Hazebrouck to Calais five French officers did not exchange two words; from Calais to Abbéville thirty who did not speak. I spoke to an artillery captain, grumbling at the slow progress of the train. He answered in English:

"Many troops moving!"

Then silence.

At Amiens there entered a civilian. It was on a Saturday towards eight o'clock in the morning and the train had the air of not wishing to reach Paris until after three. As I had business in Paris and should have to leave early on the Monday I asked this gentleman if I should find the banks shut, and the ministries and shops. He answered that he did not know. He was not a Parisian. He was going to Jersey to take possession of the body of a young girl who, having been drowned at Dieppe, had floated as far as that island. . . . As if there had not been enough deaths.

He began crying very unobtrusively.

But he, too, had spoken to me in English!

And then . . . silence. The officers regarded the civilian with eyes that said nothing at all. . . . I assure you that it was not gay.

At Creil there got in two ladies. They were pretty

and very well-dressed. *They* talked enough, those two. . . . Red Cross, charitable activities, colonels, families. But the officers never looked at them. Not one raised his eyes although the girls were young, very pretty and well-dressed!

But, when *we* had been going up to the Front from Rouen to Albert—and we were not going on leave like all these silent officers—we sang, we joked with young women whom we saw on the railway platforms; we kicked footballs along the corridors of the train; we climbed on the roofs of the carriages. You would have thought we were going to the Derby.

I naturally exaggerate these differences a little. This is not an article but a letter. But I am nevertheless telling you what my eyes have seen and my ears heard. And how is it to be explained?

It is not enough to say—as has been said so often—that if in England, the Germans had been established between York and Manchester, if they had seized the factories, pillaged the downs, and indulged in whatever the Hun Practices may be, we also should be gloomy, sad, taciturn. I am not talking of the civilian population of my country; I am speaking of us people out here whose life is not gay, who are expatriated, far from our homes and who suffer, I assure you, from a very real nostalgia. For, *là-bas* . . . on the Somme or in Flanders one feels one's self very forgotten, very deserted, and very, very isolated with an isolation like the isolation that is felt by . . . Oh, well, it is as if we were suspended—we, seven million men—on a carpet in the infinitudes of space. The roads which stretch out before us cease suddenly at a few furlongs from our faces—in No Man's Land. And it is very saddening to contemplate roads which suddenly end. And then the roads and paths that we have taken to get here—and which lie between ourselves and our *pays*—the nooks where we were born—are roads which we may not travel. . . . And I assure you that, just like any other men, we love our wives, our houses, our children, our parents, our ingle-nooks, our fields, our cattle and our dung-heaps. The French soldier has at least that to his advantage, that he fights at home. That is something for him, as individual. When he steps out of the trenches he is at least in the land that bore him. . . . But we . . .

I suppose that it is in order to forget, not only the Hun shells but also those other things that are dear to us, the chimney corner beside which we have so often sat chatting, the fields upon which we have labored, the herds and the woods—it is in search of the herb oblivion, that we play cricket behind Bécourt wood and go over the top kicking footballs across No Man's Land—footballs which pass over the corpses of the fallen, towards the Huns. . . . And crying "Stick it, the Welsh!"—is that weakness? Is it the source from which we draw—such as they are—what we have of tenacity and courage? I do not know.

Like myself, my dear confrère, you have known the difficulty of exactly defining the shades of differences that distinguish differing peoples. We commence by theorizing and we theorize much too soon, or else we take the opposite view to theories that have been accepted for centuries. We have had in England the nineteenth century caricaturists of the French during the Napoleonic wars which showed us the Frenchman as he was in the British popular imagination. He was a meager, famished barber who lived exclusively on frogs. And on your side you had your John Bull, as big as an ox, his belly as big as the belly of an ox, and devouring whole oxen. And you had the figure of the milord with his millions, his spleen which drove him to be suicidal. They were stupid, those caricatures, but it is impossible to allege that they were not sincere. The English who fought in France in 1815 sought for what they saw—but they found it. And the same with the French.

The same perhaps with myself. I have always considered the French a grave people, and when I came from an excited England, covered from the Isle of Anglesey to the North Foreland with patriotic and colorful placards and then found, from the Belgian frontier to Paris, a France quite without colored placards and gray, silent and preoccupied, it was natural that I should look for grave people and find them. But for me there was nothing new in finding France preoccupied, because for me France always was the France of fields, villages, woods and peasants. And the France of the peasants is a very laborious and pensive place where men labor incessantly between wood and pond or beneath the olive trees of the Midi.

For me, on the other hand the population of Great Britain has always been a town people. Well, it is the inhabitants of great cities who, work as they may, have need from time to time to go, as our saying is, on a spree—each according to his nature. And that is perhaps the reason of the differences that have so struck me, between the French Army and ourselves. The British Forces are made up preponderatingly of townsmen, the French army is an army preponderatingly peasant—for even the famous Parigots are mostly country born and bred. And the peasantry of all countries, but particularly the French peasant, is inured to confronting the harshness and the inevitable necessities of Nature. They meet them without ceasing for weeks, for months, for years—for their lifetimes. They can never escape from hardships and the contemplation of the evils of life, the bitter winds, the worms that devour the buds of whole harvests; their thoughts can never be diverted by taking a day's leave, in making puns or by that humor which is acrid and rather sad and which is yet the sovereign quality of the British Tommy. For to inscribe on an immense gray shell that is about to be fired at the Hun lines—to inscribe on that in huge whitewash letters "Love to Little Willie" may seem stupid and shocking to folk who were never *là-bas*. But human psychology is very complicated and it is certain that the reading of such inscriptions on the great shells by the stacks of which we pass along the highroads of France much lightens our hearts when we advance from Albert to La Boisselle.

Why? It is difficult to say. It is perhaps because, the shells being terrible and threatening, here is a shell that has been rendered ridiculous, a cause for joy—or even merely human. For we are all anthropomorphic—and that one sole shell can suffer itself to become the vehicle for humor, that is sufficient to give to superstitious minds the idea that shells may be a little less superhuman than they seem. They are the messengers of gods athirst for blood, who proclaim their gigantic weariness but nevertheless destroy in a minute dungheaps, whole fields or all the houses of a village. But they have become a little humanized.

And it is the same for our game of cricket which we played behind Bécourt Wood amongst the giant thistles, hidden in thick dust and concealing in turn the bodies of so many of our dead. But I assure you, my dear comrade, that landscape—of Bécourt, Fricourt, Mametz, Martinpuich and the rest—was not gay. It was July and the sun let down its rays upon those broad valleys, upon the dust and the smoke that mounted to the heavens and upon the black and naked woods. And it did not smile, that territory. No; Nature herself there seemed terrible and threatening—in that domain where Destiny who is blind and implacable, must manifest herself to several million human souls. . . . And then we played cricket there—and, all of a sudden that threatening and superhuman landscape became . . . just a cricket field.

For an Intellectual a field will be always just a field whether there descend upon it shells, thunderbolts—or merely tennis balls. But for us a countryside where we have played cricket becomes less affrighting and we shall there pass our days more contentedly in spite of the bones that there lie hidden amongst the thistles. It is stupid; it is even, if you will, sacrilege. But that is how we are made—we others who are not the intelligentsia and who issue forth from the great cities to go upon bloody wars. I, I have felt like that, down there, behind Bécourt Wood of a July evening during the Somme push in 1916.

And I remain always yours affectionately

G.

And I beg you to observe that all the persons who spoke to me between Steenewerck and Paris used English. That is already something.

And *I* beg you to observe that when Gringoire is moving his prose up to its most emotional pitch he employs a 'Hun' expression. For the phrase 'the herb oblivion' is merely the literal translation of the almost hackneyed German expression: *"Das Kraut Vergessenheit."*

—*Note by the Compiler.*

PART TWO

CERTAIN INTERIORS

The old houses of Flanders,
They watch by the high cathedrals;
They overtop the high town halls;
They have eyes, mournful, tolerant and sardonic for the ways
of men
In the high, white, tiled gables.

The rain and the night have settled down on Flanders;
It is all wet darkness, you can see nothing.

Then those old eyes, mournful, tolerant and sardonic,
Look at great sudden red lights,
Look upon the shades of the cathedrals,
And the golden rods of the illuminated rain.

And those old eyes,
Very old eyes that have watched the ways of men for generations,
Close for ever.
The high, white shoulders of the gables
Slouch together for a consultation,
Slant drunkenly over in the lea of the flaming cathedrals.

They are no more the old houses of Flanders.

VIII

"Maisie"

[It has occurred to the writer—or let us rather say, "the compiler," that, as concerns this section of this work, it would be safe to let Gringoire speak for himself. The paraphernalia of inverted commas interspersed with indirect speech is apt to be wearisome to a reader. It is difficult—nay, it might even prove dangerous—to the compiler. For who shall say what powerful enemies the present writer might not make by omitting inverted commas and appearing to speak for himself? So it seems more just to let the rather testy poet speak for himself.

For undoubtedly, when speaking of certain matters, Gringoire was—nay, he is!—apt to become testy. Let us excuse him by saying that he bore a good deal of strain during the late war—as was apt to be the position of any public, or quasi-public man, caught between the attentions of the cheap press and what he considered to be his duty to the State.

Of course, this section is a rendering. It does not pretend to record words exactly as Gringoire spoke. It is, rather, a résumé of conversations of an evening when the writer—or rather the compiler—was privileged to be housed by Gringoire. It was, by then, late summer or early autumn.

The Gingerbread Cottage by that date resembled less one of the ruins of the Flanders front that Gringoire so feelingly describes. For to tell the truth, that was what it had very nearly resembled at the time of our Easter visit. When Gringoire had entered it in the early spring, there had been certainly the wave-marks of inundations and half-inches of mud on the brick floors. He had come down with his valise contents, his camp-bed, a knife and fork, a paraffin stove, and a gallon of oil, determined, as he puts it, to dig himself in in the face of destiny. At Easter we had seen him a little too early in the process for people who had not for the last four or five years lived with furniture made of bully-beef cases or whatever they are called.

But by mid-September, when the greater portion of the following section was compiled, either Gringoire's views as to the æsthetic value of bully-beef chairs and tables had changed as he got further from the atmosphere of camps, or Mme. Sélysette had softened the asperities of his nature in the matter of preference of dugouts to drawing rooms—or else, truly, he was acting up to his ideals. That one hesitates to believe: for who can believe that any human soul can act up to his professed ideals—or that the ideals which he professes have any relation to his motives?

Still, Gringoire was a poet. And the writer remembers remonstrating with him as to the amount of work he was putting into the Gingerbread Cottage and the garden. Said the writer: Gringoire should remember that all this whitewashing, papering, glazing the windows, digging out of foundations, and fertilizing an abandoned and ill-treated garden would, in the end, profit only the landlord—who was a very bad landlord, even as bad landlords go. For, as would be the case with poets, Gringoire had no lease of any kind. . . .

But Gringoire only looked at the writer with that vague and unseeing glance that is one of the properties of some poets. And he answered: though of course it was not an answer: He was not a small hatter, a market-gardener, a farmer, a tradesman, or any sort of profit-and-loss person. He was intent simply on making his sanctuary smile a little in the sunlight and on comforting an old building that had been very shabbily used by evil sorts of men. . . .

At any rate, they had scrambled together some old and rather attractive "bits," a grandfather's chair or so, carpets for the sitting room, colored rush mats for the floor of the sleeping apartments. They had painted and polished with beeswax and turpentine, and there would, as like as not, be some flowers on the dining table which was of rough oak—and coffee after a full dinner.

The primitive "note" remained, of course, about the establishment, and it was hardly the place to which you would have asked for a week-end a delicate city madam; a Guards' Major; or a young actress about to become famous. But on bright days the garden smiles in the sun, and the Gingerbread Cottage has a colored and—as Gringoire would say—a *soigné* aspect. Yes, certainly it appeared to be cared for, poor battered old thing, as old people sometimes appear to be cared for in almshouses.

So Gringoire affronts the winter. And, if during that season the wolf does not get him; or if his patience does not give out—as is the case with poets; or if the bad landlord does not eject him in order to reap the profits of his improvements—for he has no lease! —he will continue his patchings, his experiments with unusual manures, and his attempts to ameliorate the breed of potatoes. And that is all the writer will say about him.

For the rest, he speaks for himself, much as he spoke of an evening, with his mild but occasionally bitter and furious eyes; with his usually tranquil, but occasionally furiously gesticulating hands. For, the writer, or rather the compiler, having compared notes with Mme. Sélysette, who has heard Gringoire's stories very, very often, the compiler is satisfied that it is a fair rendering of the poet-warrior's conversation. It will be found to be disfigured, even in this, as it were, censored version, by unfortunate attacks on many persons and institutions that are usually considered exempt from—or at any rate dangerous to—assault. But what it contains is not half as violent as what Gringoire wished the compiler to set down as his opinions. The compiler, however, has friends who can be grieved; a pocket that can be affected by the law of libel; a position with reviewers that is his stock in trade. So Gringoire, who could not write prose but wished to air his opinions, and the compiler, who wished to air the poet's opinions but did not wish to lose friends, money, or position in the process, agreed upon the autobiographical passages that follow.]

Gringoire speaks:

At some period of the war, I found myself in a certain interior. It was August—hushed by the presence at the doors of functionaries, elderly, gray, like bishops, wearing evening dress. And one had the sense that, standing at ease, on the steps of great portals, opening onto immense staircases, that one had ascended in stony twilights, past bistre-blue frescoes. Suisses, in cocked hats with great white gloves and silver swords, symbolized the military ideals of Ministries, just as, in the Vatican, obsolete artillerymen, hussars, pikemen, symbolize a vanished temporal power. For, what would the Suisses do if the Enemy or a Revolution should chance to pay a call on them?

I presume they would extend enormous, cotton-gloved fingers for visiting cards, which they would hand to commissionaires in glass boxes; the cards would be sent by pages, upstairs to the episcopal butlers, who, after meditating for forty minutes, would warily convey them, over the soft State carpets, past the decorous but rich, State-purchased pictures suspended over the blue-gray, State-woven tapestries, to the high door of polished mahogany. There the bishop-butlers would pause, with the air of priests listening outside shrines, with a hand on the engraved, polished, mounted, ormolu door-handles. . . .

But what, during those sixty-four minutes would be the proceedings of the lieutenant of Uhlans, with his twenty men behind him; or the leader of the sans-culottes, communards, syndicalists. . . ? The lances might be dripping with blood; bread, dripping too, might be decorating the points of pikes, or paraffin from the oil cans. Probably they would not wait until the blood or the oil dried on the sarcophagus-tiles of the Ministerial Salle des Pas Perdus or until the great hotel slowly and resignedly disappeared in flames with that curious air of weary acquiescence that buildings have when, having borne for many years with human follies, wisdoms, or labors, they fall to the ground before human madness. Probably they would not wait —the Uhlans, the sans-culottes, or the Pétroleuses. They are an impatient people.

But, of course, the reader will say, in the great courtyard before the Ministry, are many, many gendarmes, standing about with their hands behind their backs and slightly protuberant bellies. (Otherwise they would be *là bas!*) But they have good eyes. They would know a Lieutenant of Uhlans by his uniform, and they know how to use their revolvers. And amongst the gendarmes lounge several civilian men of queer, specialized miens. Their pockets bulge just slightly, in odd ways, and brushing their legs are the *chiens de bergers Alsaciens* (it used to be *Allemands*) the large, elegant dogs with brown fur, like ladies' sable coats and the intelligent pointed ears. . . . It is the business of these apparently civilian agents to know the leaders of sans-culottes, syndicalists, communards, and *Actions* this or that. The pretty, friendly, high-stepping dogs with their sable coats would be at the sans-culottes' throats at the merest chirrup of their masters' lips, and from the so very slightly bulging pockets light handcuffs would whip out. The revolvers also would go off. . . .

And, still more, the reader will say, in the little, painted, upright boxes stand little men with red trousers and blue coats and tricolored worsted galloons, and long, dull-looking rifles, and very, very long

Rosalies. . . . They are probably just the very newest recruits with sad, boyish faces. But they know enough to say the French for "Halt, who are you?" in Breton accents, and to let off the old, long guns, and to stick Rosalie, with a grunt, through the entrails of a Uhlan lieutenant, and to call out the Guard. . . . And, too, there is a half-battalion of the 101st Regiment, whose accent reeks of garlic, olive oil, and the meridional sun, passing along the boulevard before the tricolor that droops over the porte-cochère. . . .

So—like the very heart of an onion, under many, many wrappings, in sanctuary, how very, very far from the mud of the onion-trench, bearded, in a dark coat, with a bright spot of a button; with sharp, apprehending nods coming as quickly as winks and silences as quickly as either; behind the polished mahogany door with the gilt handle and the ormolu finger-plates; at a Buhl table, with a glass vase full of Malmaison carnations, a bronze reproduction of the Winged Victory, and two great pictures of Norman peasants, the one by Bastien Lepage and the other by Jean François Millet—sits the Minister whose mere wink to some one, whose whisper to some one else, whose instruction to another, whose order—and so on

—has brought one from green fields littered with bully beef-tins, wire, mud-trodden cartridge cases, rat runs—and the rest of it! He will thank you for past services; tactfully suggest that it might reinforce some department of the *moral* of some department or other of humanity if M. le Capitaine would suspend his military ardors in order to write so and so and so and so in such and such an organ or to say this and that in a certain quarter. And one can also produce not truly a great effect but some, by talking in a certain way, in the mess of one's regiment even. Certainly in Quartiers Généraux . . .

He will listen deferentially whilst you voice certain objections: to write so and so one must have leave—leave in both the English and the French sense of "permission." And leaves are difficult things to obtain. Besides, one does not want leave. For certain reasons! . . . One is like that. *L'on est poète:* cranky, unreasonable. An all-powerful Minister cannot get into the soul of a crank. Not his Seneschals, or the Suisses, or the Gendarmes, or the Agents, or the Sentinels can help him to that. *Quand on est poète* one requires—one requires a little reëntrant, with water—a little stream, indicated by a wavy line in blue pencil; copses, indicated by dotted-in round o's with tails to them; rushes, indicated by hieroglyphs like the section of a hairbrush; a gingerbread cottage, for which the symbol is a hatched in square.—One requires those. And also one requires a temporary respite from the attentions of one's friends and of destiny. For that, as far as I know, military topography has no symbol—unless it be a white handkerchief on the end of Rosalie.

His Excellency remains polite—deferential even. Still, it could no doubt be arranged, he will remark. It is important to get certain things said. . . . And who could say it better than . . .

For myself—on the occasion which I am adumbrating, I was thinking of ferrets. So that, by a concentration of ideas, at a given point I once said to such a Minister: Of course there is the First Line Transport. . . . And, in my mind's eye, against the gilt frame of the immense Bastien Lepage—or it may have been on this occasion a Marie Bashkirtseff—arose the image of a Connaught Hut, with the rain beating on the roof and the autumn wind reaching the flames of candles stuck in bottles and bearing in the odor of stable hartshorn from the long horse standings. And the Welsh Rabbit made of cheese, onions, Flemish beer, and herrings straight from Bailleul—though God knows when they came from the autumnal sea. And hooch. And several obese, tranquil, entirely capable officers with feet for the moment in carpet slippers. And the table utensils borrowed from the Y.M.C.A. pushed aside on a corner of the trestle table; and a cheap pad of letter paper, a copying ink pencil, and the mind of the poet functioning in the flicker of the guttering candles at the dictates of the Minister seated beneath the Jean François Millet picture at the Buhl table with the Malmaison carnations in a smoked glass vase and the miniature reproduction of the Winged Victory in bronze with a delicate, artificially produced patina. And the lower part of the poet is wedged into a bully-beef case that has had one side taken out and that has been wire-nailed into an egg-box to form an armchair. And, in the dim gloom, at one elbow stands a dripping Divisional runner with a buff memo from ordnance to say that Mills Bombs for the —— Battalion are on the Scherpenberg and must be taken down to Kemmel Château by four ack emma; and at the other elbow stands a Divisional Orderly with a copy of orders on which in red ink is marked the information that Division will move down the line by the road by Dranoutre—Neuve Eglise—Westoutre-Plugstreet—Pont-de-Nieppe—Armentières. In full sight of the Hun trenches, by God!—beginning with one's own battalion, of which A. Company will march from such and such a spot at 5:30 to be followed by D, C, and B boys at half-hour intervals. And to be shelled to Hell!

And the transport officer, whose business it is to manage these matters, is away for thirty-six hours to arrange for a Divisional Horse Show in the field behind the Convent! And your poet is A. O. I. C. (Acting Officer in Charge of) Transport, and Billeting officer for the Battalion and O. I. C. (Officer in Charge of) Divisional Canteen and God knows what all. And Officer in Charge of *moral* of a certain section of humanity to whom it would be a good thing if certain things would be said in polished prose! And when the poet springing up exclaims to the night:

"To H—— with the b——y Mills Bombs and the bumph and the b——rs and all the whole execrable show," the Battalion Orderly, a fair, cheeky boy who knows one, exclaims:

"Ker wooly woo, sir, say la Gair!"

And indeed, the interiors of *la guerre* were much

like that. But how is His Excellency the Minister of this or that department to know what is passing in your mind? He will just write on a note pad, look up, exclaim, "Que dîtes-vous? First Line? . . . But is it tranquil, that?" [1]

I don't know what I answered. I believe I must have screamed with laughter—because I really wanted some ferrets very badly, and because, in the vestibule of an immense hotel I had left my publisher in charge of a little girl with dark curls tied with pale blue ribbons, singularly self-possessed manners, and rather prominent underclothing that appeared to be an inverted bouquet of lace. That is to say I had left my publisher —who is deaf—with the little girl. And I was in charge of the little girl, who, just before my having to hurry to the Ministry, had devoured thirteen oysters, half a cantaloupe melon with a quarter of a pound of sugar, and a *Coupe Jacques*. So I was, really, wonder-

[1] For the benefit of those curious in these matters, I ask our compiler to print in the Envoi some prose in my own original French. It will serve for a curiosity. It appeared in a Swiss Review during the war and was part of somewhat considerable, and generally agitated, labors. Some poems which I wrote in almost exactly the circumstances given above, for recitation to French troops, have been lost either by our own or the French ministry of propaganda. An article about Alsace-Lorraine was "lost in the post"; another, repeating it, was suppressed by our own Ministry of Information as being too favorable to the claims of one of our Allies. It is, of course, difficult to be a poet in times of war.

ing what Maisie would be like when I returned to the Hotel de l'Opéra. It sounds mad—but it is just the true truth.

I know that, at that stage, I did not please His Excellency. He frowned twice. Once when I laughed because he asked if a Connaught hut at the base of the Salient was a tranquil place in which to write poems. He also frowned when—as I have, I know, elsewhere related, but I do not know where—he having asked me, *"En quoi il me pouvait être utile?"* I answered, *"Si Votre Excellence me pourrait trouver des furets!"*

You see, I had been carefully instructed by friends with one eye to my commercial future. The Minister was sure to ask in what way he could be of service to me. I was to reply—to hint ever so delicately—that if I had a ribbon to stick on my coat, writing poems, even in a Connaught hut, would be easy. But I couldn't do it. Even if I had not been concerned with ferrets that I couldn't get and with Maisie, who had been far too easy to come by, I couldn't have done it. I had been instructed that the ribbon awaited me; I had only to stretch out a hand to become an Officer of Something or Other. I don't know whether I ever have. I suppose not.

Anyhow, His Excellency frowned when I asked for ferrets. He might have been more sympathetic if I had asked him to take off my hands a little girl of eight, with the American manners appropriate to the age of thirteen, who, half an hour before had eaten thirteen oysters, half a melon, and a quarter of a pound of sugar that had come from Geneva in her *malles,* and a *Coupe Jacques;* who had been kidnapped by the lake in a carriage and pair, the night before, or perhaps two nights before; and whose father, the kidnapper, had left her in my charge just after breakfast and had then disappeared. There was also a very French maid—in hysterics. And I didn't even know their names.

Yes; H. E. might have been more sympathetic if I had mentioned the child alone in the vestibule—or possibly with the publisher. But at the mention of the ferrets, he became positively glacial: *"Quoi,"* he asked. "What is a ferret?"

I said that *ferrets sont des petits animaux qui mangent les rats.* But his face remained like a dead wall. I *know* he thought I was drunk. I was so certain of it, then, that I stammered, and the interview dissolved in the embarrassed emotions passing from him to me and from me to him. He touched a button and said he would telephone to the Jardin des Plantes. But I don't suppose he did.

You see: it was almost a drop too much in my cup —to be plunged straight into "What Maisie Knew," which is a book by Henry James. It was too much bewilderment. . . . Supposing the—as I understood—too brilliant and vociferous mother who was understood to like a "violinist fellow", should be bursting, with wide gestures, through the aperture frailly closed by glass hotel-doors that whirled bewilderingly whilst I was at the Ministry. . . . And it might, I understood, well be like that.

How the incident ended, however, I cannot say, since, upon my return to the hotel, the child and her companion had disappeared. That is to say, they had left in the hotel bus for the *Gare du Nord*. So I hope they got safely to England. I never heard: and, since I have forgotten even the names, I suppose I never shall.

It was, no doubt, the sort of thing that was happening all over the world just as usual, but it was queer —and intensely worrying—to be brought so violently and so much against one's poor will into an atmosphere of international passions, excursions, lawsuits for the possession of children, and the like. And anyhow, the worry of it probably spoilt my career; which was no doubt a good thing. Anyhow, I hope that Maisie, in the custody of kind old aunts, somewhere in Sussex, is prattling to a benevolent but bewildered butler about Mamma, who went to heaven by the cog-wheel railway, via Montreux. Or I suppose it would be better for her if she had forgotten Mamma.

Yes: I suppose it was all going on. And I rather fancy I found the going-on-ness of it all a little appalling. Paris, indeed, was so much more just Paris out of the season, than London, in those days, appeared to be London, either during or out of the season. It was in a way touching; it was also, in a way, disheartening. I remember—and I say "I remember" advisedly, since such an immense number of things blotted themselves out and only crop up in suddenly vivid pictures like that of Maisie whom I had completely forgotten until the day before yesterday, and who now again exists extraordinarily brightly in the hotel vestibule saying: *"Ils me disent que Maman est partie pour le ciel.* It is very droll. But what tram do I take *pour le ciel?"* I remember, then, being on a balcony with an immense stone balustrade, in the black night with a number of

French officers who were all polite—but cold. It was, certainly, during the *entr'acte* of Delibes' *Lakme.* I fancy the theater was the Comédie Française, but I don't know, because I had been taken there by a staff officer, and in those days in France one was moved about so without volition of one's own that one didn't, necessarily, much notice where one went or how one got there. Where it was a duty to notice, one noticed —railway stations in their sequence, streams, contours. But it was rather a toss-up whether anything more than little bits, like etchings or vignettes, got through to one's private psychology. I take this to have been the case with most men in our army. We were, as soldiers, both naïf and engrossed.

With the French, it was different. They appeared to be so much older, in their work as in their leisures. They seemed to go to war, as they went to *Lakme,* so much more as connoisseurs. So, on that balcony, I had the feeling of a very definite frigidity. I could have talked rather floridly about *les gloires de la France,* the ultimate aims of the war. I doubt if the French officers could. They had exhausted the topic during forty menaced years.

So they talked, as it happens, mostly of the fine

work that had been done by their territorials—old men, fathers of families, and grandfathers who were patching away at the trenches, making roads under fire, laboriously laboring amidst great dangers and beyond their strength that the years had sapped.

The balcony of the theater was a cube of blackness; down below there appeared to be an old, small, square market-place. Paris, of course, was in darkness, out of deference to Zeppelins and airplanes, so that it was all a heavy, velvety black beneath a pallid sky. Houses, squares, rose up on three sides; the immense black bulk of the theater seemed to press on one's back as one is pressed upon, on narrow paths, by the walls of precipices in the night. One had a sense that the inside of this building was flooded with translucent rays, in which, over the light parquet of long floors, in the *salons de réception,* men moved quietly, with slightly outstretched hands emphasizing points in their discourse to the women on their arms. Theaters function with a sense of style in Paris. But the old, tall houses round the market gave the idea that they were solidly black throughout; only in the old empty rooms, over the creaking floors, mice would rustle in the pallid gleams from the old windows.

I do not mean to say that the houses were really like that inside: for houses are queer things, and queerer still when they grow old, with malices, obstinacies, benevolences of their own. And, as is the case with men, their physiognomies are misleading. So, though one had the sense that below there was a market-place with carts and tilted hoods awaiting the day and that the houses were old and empty, it may have been all untrue to fact, though it is likely enough in Paris where there are so many old, moldering, and damp-streaked façades and courtyards.

I wonder if most people have as strongly as I the feeling that houses have, not so much immortal souls, as tempers, queernesses, and the power to be malicious or benevolent. I daresay most people have that sense up to a point, for it is common enough to walk with a friend, more particularly at dawn, where there are few human beings about to detract from the spell, past, say, a terrace of houses not all alike. A blind will be up; another and another, half drawn down; four or five others, all green, will be at various heights behind the closed window-glasses. And your friend will say:

"That house appears to be winking; that other is

gnashing green teeth!" So that your friend will be attributing faces at least to the houses. No doubt he will also connote individualities.

The effect of the coming of the war, for me, was to enhance the feeling until it became almost an obsession. Just as trees and fields appeared to dread the contamination of alien presences, so with buildings. Only with buildings—and more particularly with houses—the feeling was very much enhanced. They seemed to dread not only contaminations, but pains, violations, physical shames, and dissolution in fire.

I do not mean that this feeling was new to me or came with the coming of the war. On the contrary, it was a feeling familiar enough in France. Long before the war it was difficult to go to Northern France—and it was impossible to visit Paris—without seeing, or having the attention drawn to, buildings that have been struck by shells, that have solid cannon balls embedded in their walls, to façades riddled by musketry or charred by one incendiarism or another. In Paris, there were mostly relics of 1870-71; elsewhere the solid cannon balls, as like as not, were once our own. But somehow that seemed normal: those were the danger zones of a race. If members of a civilized people, like the French, choose to occupy marches—zones set against barbarians, like ourselves and the Huns—the buildings they set up in those regions must suffer. They must suffer as children do who are taken into perils aboard ship; or like dogs whose masters adventure with them into fields of fire.

It was, therefore, in the southern and central regions of France that, before the war, I had most strangely the feeling—that feeling of affrighted buildings. It came to me one day in a broad French landscape, somewhere, I imagine, just south of Lyons. Perhaps it was in Orange—or possibly in Tarascon. At any rate, it was just after the close of the Agadir "incident".

I don't know that I had taken the Agadir incident very seriously. In fact, I hadn't taken it seriously at all. The Prime Minister of today had made at the Guildhall a speech that one regarded as one regarded any other flamboyant speech—and that was the end of it. I never imagined that we should do our duty to civilization if it came to the point. I never imagined, indeed, that France herself would stand up.

We came, at that date, of a generation that lived in the shadow of the ghosts of Bismarck, Moltke, and

William I—in the shadow of memories of the siege of Paris. Prussia appeared no doubt detestable—but she was so omnipotent that we hardly cared to think about her even for the purpose of detesting her. Will you remember, oh Gringoire *fils* that shall be?

Probably Gringoire *fils* will not remember: that is why I find it necessary to recapitulate at this point. Prussia, then, was there, like something ominous but irremovable. One might say that the world, like some stout old garment, was a good world—but it had upon it a grease-stain that neither petrol nor spirits would eradicate; just as you might say that your postal service or train system were good, ignoring the fact that officials were brutal in manner; or that your God was a good God, although He insisted on being fed with babies roasted alive. Something like that.

On the day after Agadir, then, I had come through Lorraine—the two Lorraines, of which one was bubbling like a pot with men all in gray, the other pullulating like an over-ripe cheese with men all in blue, with baggy, scarlet breeches. One had been lost in an immense, pushing, silent crowd at the *Gare de l'Ouest* —an immense, silent, rather grim crowd in blue, with worsted adornments, long rifles slung over the backs, untidy haversacks. At the bureaux of the station were innumerable women. They gesticulated, waved to unseen units in that tired crowd; they cried out; they wept for joy.

But that produced no particular effect. The French are an impressionable and a noisy people. So the women called out. The silent soldiery were no doubt tired after the autumn manoeuvres. That was perhaps why they were so grim.

But somewhere, just after that, in some view near a Southern or Central town—as I have said, it may have been Lyons or Orange; no town that particularly mattered, near the Loire, perhaps, or the Rhone—amidst rolling country where the harvest was already in and there were stubble fields and new straw thatching—suddenly, out of all those hundreds of thousands of soldiery, I remembered one. He was a little recruit—"joining up" as we learned to say later. He was shoved into a first-class carriage somewhere near Meaux because the train was so full, and there, in a corner seat, with the blue-gray landscape going past, he sat, as if lifeless, the tears dropping down his cheeks. His rifle, haversack, packages, tin cans, slings, and things of which, then, one didn't recognize the importance, had been thrown in after him by a guard, and, in among them, he sat desolate.

In the carriage there had been besides myself two old French people—an old gentleman with a white Napoleon, and an old, feeble lady, in a rather queer black bonnet. I have an idea that they were French Protestants. There were also other people: but they formed only a chorus.

For the old man, in kindly, but very thin tones, began to talk to the little recruit, the old lady echoing each of his speeches:

"The beds for a poor little recruit are hard?"—"The beds are hard!"—"The haricot soup is thin?"—"Ah, yes, a very watery potage."—"Ah! Ah! Yes," said the listeners.—"The marchings are long; the drills difficult; the rifles heavy."—"Yes: heavy are the rifles!"—"Ah! Ah! Yes . . ."—"And the little recruit is away from home for three long years!"—"Yes, three years!"—"Ah! Ah! Ah! Three so very long years!"—"The little recruit comes from the Midi—the South!"—"The Midi! The South!"—"Ah! Ah! The South with sun and cypress hedges and the *champs d'oliviers* and the Mistral."—"From Orange! From quite near Orange . . . Ah! Ah! Orange . . ." And there he was, going to Lille. . . . In the northwest: over against the frontier. . . .

Being then "quite near Orange" a few days later—yes, it was Orange!—and looking out from the heights of the Roman Theater over the little town and the flat, commonplace country, I remembered suddenly the little recruit. I think that is how the mind really works, linking life together, for, later I shall tell you how, on the balcony of the Comédie Française, I remembered suddenly Private ——, an old, nearly toothless Tommy of a Kitchener's battalion of the Lincolnshires in the baths which had been established in the old mill at Albert—and also Lt. Morgan of my own regiment, an officer who had spent a very hard life in Canada, and who was killed walking up a communication trench on his first day in the line.

So, at Orange, before the war, I remembered suddenly the little recruit in his blue, with his worsted adornments, sitting like a statue of utter grief whilst the green-gray country, of northwest France, swept past behind him. The country over which his image suddenly superimposed itself was browner; in flat fields, the queer twigs of the vineyards appeared untidy. I fancy the Alps were in the distance. But there were stacks and roofs. And, it was, for me, just country. That is to say, I attached to that countryside no particular legends, traditions, or fables of story. It might be Provence—or it might not. But when I saw, as it were, through the image of the recruit, the stacks, the roofs, of the little farm buildings or of the little town, it seemed to me that they were all crouching down, motionless, but ready to tremble, as partridges crouch amid the stubble when beaten away over the ridge.

I don't want unduly to labor the point—but I am not yet certain that I have made it. You see, that queer and sinister feeling came to me just because of that carriageful of French people. It was not so much because the little recruit had wept. I daresay that, as a conscript, he was bad material. But it was because the old gentleman and all the others in the carriage had known the hard beds, the thin soups, the heavy rifles, and the drag of the pack-straps on the shoulders . . . and the long absences from the little homes that seemed now to cower among the stubble fields. For there was no house in all that landscape whose women hadn't known the suspense of absences; there was no stack whose builder hadn't at one time gone, or come back.

And there was not one, of all those objects, that did not dread—that, for forty long years had not dreaded—the hard footsteps, the shames, the violations, or the incendiary fires of conquerors who should come from "beyond Lille on the frontier".

And it was at that moment that, suddenly, it became a conscious proposition in my mind—definite and formulated—that, first and before everything else, we must have in the world assured nooks and houses that never cowered and trembled—houses of which one could never by any possibility think that they would cower and tremble.

That, of course, is militarism. I am sorry that it has crept in.

IX

The Water Mill

Said Gringoire on another day:

During one of the innumerable periods of long waiting that seemed inseparable from our advances whether on the Somme or elsewhere, it occurred to me that that would be a good opportunity to see what books really would bear reading—would, that is to say, stand up against the facts of a life that was engrossing and perilous. I wrote, therefore, on the spur of the moment, a postcard, to a bookseller, since I had no friends on whose generosity I cared to trespass. I asked him to send me: Turgeniev's "Fathers and Children", Flaubert's "Trois Contes", Mallarmé's "Après-Midi d'un Faune", Anatole France's "Histoire Comique", or "Thaïs", "Youth", by Joseph Conrad, "What Maisie Knew", by Henry James, and "Nature in Downland", by W. H. Hudson. I received them all except the last, which was out of print, and I found that I could read them all with great engrossment except the book, whichever it was, by Anatole France. That one was so frail and tenuous in its appeal that it failed to hold my attention at all, and I have forgotten its name.—I hasten to add that I regarded M. France at that date as a Pro-German, so my impatience may not have been altogether because of its literary qualities.

It was whilst I was reading "What Maisie Knew" that I got leave to go with another officer and have a bath in Albert. So I took the volume under my arm. It wasn't really a coincidence—that I should be reading that book. I suppose it wasn't really a coincidence that I should meet Maisie in the flesh.

For, if one was to meet Maisie anywhere, it would be precisely in the white vestibule of a Paris hotel—and, if any one was to be confided in by one or other of her distracted parents, the episode being international, and the parent in possession British, the person to be confided in *would* be one in the uniform of His Britannic Majesty, and of substantial appearance. "What Maisie Knew," again, happened to be the first book by the late Mr. James that I ever read—and, if it hadn't happened to be the first, it would still have remained—and it does still remain for me—the book by that very great writer that most "matters". For your benefit, if you "don't know your James," I may as well say that this is the story of a child moving amongst elemental passions that are veiled. But, of course, elemental passions can never be veiled enough not to get through to the consciousness, if not to the intelligence of the child in the house. So, in an atmosphere of intrigues, divorces, prides, jealousies, litigations, conducted as these things are conducted in this country, by what it is convenient to call "the best people", Maisie always "knows". She knows all about concealed relationships, as she knows all about intrigues, processes, and the points of view of old family servants. It is, of course, a horrible book, but it is very triumphantly true. . . .

The Tommies' bathing place at Albert was in an old mill under the shadow of a tall factory chimney at which the Huns were perpetually firing shells. As far as I know, they never hit it—but they made a nice desolation in the immediately adjacent houses. The mill, at the fork of a road, had been turned into a series of sheds and compartments, in which there were shower baths and baths with hot and cold water in very wet cubicles where you had duckboards underfoot. There were Neissen or other boilers somewhere under the ramshackle building, so that steam always filtered through and hung over the old tiles of the roof. The other ranks of various battalions had their bathing parades there at stated hours, so that officers could only get a bath in between whiles or after hours.

It was a hot day, very dusty, with the clouds from the white rubble, which was all that there was of the center of the town, and after we had wandered, I and another officer, round about the rubbish heaps, and past long-closed shops that offered us, on metal placards, bicycles, chocolates, and furniture polish, by makers well-known in France, we decided to wait in the bath itself till the battalion in possession, which was the last of the day, should have finished its ablutions. In a tiny, shuttered shop we had bought, for A Company's mess, a small melon, five lemons, and half a bushel of windfall apples. The shop was just to the east of the Cathedral, and we went over the empty Presbytery. One of the floors was a great litter of books—Latin texts mostly. One I noticed was a 17th century edition of Livy—1652, I think. Another was a copy of Voragine's recension of the "Golden Legend"—but whether or no it was a valuable edition, I don't know. We left the books on the floor—out of indifference, so as not to commit sacrilege and because we had already to carry a small, netted melon, six lemons, and half a bushel of apples between us. Under my arm, moreover, I had "What Maisie Knew" in the expensive, collected edition, and we had also towels and soap. So there, in the long, dark, but not cool room, just as they had been tumbled out of the shelves, probably by the Germans, the books lay with rays of sunlight from the closed *persiennes* falling across broken backs, exposed leaves, half-turned title-pages. . . .

Whilst we were passing under the immense Madonna and Child that hung over the Cathedral steps, a Hun plane dropped a couple of bombs right into the body of the church. They made pretty loud pops, and overhead our own Archies were popping away too. But what was really interesting to hear was the sifting tinkle of broken stained-glass of the windows that went on rustling, tinkling, sifting, and rustling down into the rubble in the body of the church until we were out of earshot.

I don't mean to say that we hurried away. There

was nowhere to hurry to. But the German heavy battery that had the town under its especial care was beginning to send in its evening group of shells. As far as I can remember, at that time they let off six 5-2's at about 10:15 A.M.; six at 1:15 P.M., and six more just after 6:00 P.M. with an apparently unimaginative regularity, and usually at the same localities—the morning six falling about the desolated Place in front of the church, the lunchtime contribution in the houses along the main street. Our Second Battalion had thirty-two casualties in one room from one shell of the midday group. The evening six usually fell in the fields on the Ancre side of the town.

So we desired to get under a roof—not that a roof is any particular protection against high-explosive shells, but simply to get something between one's self and the sky. For at times, of an evening, when one was tired, a pellucid sky would be a disagreeable thing. You didn't know what sort of iron shard would not be coming between the light bars of blue and the bars of light dove color. Your flesh, too, felt very soft to set itself up against iron shards. And, at the moment, we were tired with the walk over the thistles of the downland and the thin air and the heat and the chalk dust. And one wanted a read in one's book!

The by-streets were amazingly quiet; closed houses, shuttered shops, mostly unhurt; not a soul was in the blazing sunlight; not a cloud was in the sky; only, in the dust of the road three cats were motionlessly intent on love. We knocked on a closed door of the old mill. I found myself, having passed several darkish, steaming rooms in which the white nudity of many men showed against the blue-gray of flannel shirts, and the drab colors of steam-damped khaki in the shadow—I found myself in an armchair, in a very tall, quiet room. I had a sense that there was a tall, slim bookcase, a great table covered with dirty copies of English funny periodicals, and empty, cardboard fag-packets. . . . But I was sitting, really, in Kensington Gardens in the broad, open turfed way that slopes from the Round Point to the Serpentine. And there was a murmuring couple, by a tree trunk, upon green penny chairs. (I don't know that I wasn't one-half of the couple.) And Maisie was playing with Mrs. Wicks, three trees off, and Beale Farange, a little too florid, flaming and bearded, to be really one of the best people, was bearing down upon them—or was it us?

—in the shadow of the well-behaved foliage under the polite skies.

I was vaguely conscious of voices. My companion was talking to some one else—about some battalion of some regiment; about some division, not ours; about the nature of the trenches in front of *Bazentin-le-Petit.* But, at any rate, for the moment, the fictitious-real had got so much the upper hand of the real-real that I was as engrossed as any schoolboy reading Ivanhoe in the twilight. It is a good tribute to pay the master. He was dying then.

But I was vaguely unhappy too—unhappy about it all. I don't mean that I was unhappy with the ire of the moralist—for I never set up to be a moralist. Only I felt the queer uneasiness that, in those days, one was beginning to feel when one came in contact with civilians.

One began to hear hollow voices, sounding portentous through closed shutters.

"Fall in there! A Company on the right. Towels on the left arm. Number off!"—voices coming from the roadway. And one looked up from one's book, thinking the time had come for one's bath. There existed again the tall room, with grayish wallpaper;

the atmosphere of steam; the tall window; the tall bookcase, whose panes, behind thin, curved mahogany divisions showed a faded, stretched curtain of torn green silk. The table was less littered than it had been. It had a dusty, red baize cover, much stained with ink. I suppose this was the miller's office. I don't know what had become of my companion. He was a restless, energetic boy, always on the jump. Whilst I had been in the broad avenue in Kensington, he had probably pressed until they had got him a bath-cubicle cleaned and ready. At any rate, a very old Tommy of the Lincolns, toothless, whitehaired, with tunic undone and tarnished buttons, told me I must still wait whilst my bath was preparing.

He said I was mistaken in thinking that he was a noncombatant permanently in charge of the baths. He was just a Tommy of the Lincolns; he had come straight out of the trenches in front of *Bazentin-le-Petit* the night before. Five days before that they had relieved us in the same trenches. Now another division had gone in. He had been put in charge of the baths that morning, so he hadn't had time to clean his buttons, or even his rifle. He supposed he might get *strafed* for that. Yes; it was trying, the life of the trenches for a man of his age. He was sixty-two—sixty-four—over sixty, at any rate.

I told him to stand easy, and he sat down on the other side of the large table and reached for an old pipe. Then he folded his wrinkled hands before him on the cloth, looked at me hopefully, and exclaimed: "I suppose you know the firm of Bolsover & Jupp of Golden Square. The great solicitors."

I did not know them; but when I said I did not, he appeared so distressed: "What? Not the great solicitors? To the Mansion House, the Common Council, the Tilbury and Southend Railway!"—so distressed that I had to pretend at last that I did.

"Well!" he said. "I was clerk in their office for twenty-four years!"

Twenty——four——years! He seemed to think that the statement entitled him to feel an enormous pride. No doubt it did.

He must have had a streak of the adventurous in his composition—but no one could have seemed less adventurous or more static. As he sat there, his hands, whitened by dabbling all that day in bath water, and folded before him on the dirty red baize, he looked as if he had sat there all his life and as if he would never move. He was so faded that you would not have given him credit even for the amount of sharpness necessary to a solicitor's clerk; you would have said that he was an aged shepherd on a bench outside the workhouse door. I think he was the most memorable figure of the war, for me.

Of course, one's mind is capricious in these things—but this was his biography, of which I have forgotten nothing—though I have, of course, forgotten most of his exact words. For twenty-four years clerk to Messrs. Bolsover & Jupp, this man who now was mostly preoccupied with the fact that he would be *"strafed"* for not "cleanin' 'is 'ipe . . . I mean rifle, sir!" had gone at the age of forty-eight—to Canada, to make his fortune, nothing less! He had left two sons, both married, in London. He and his "missus" worked in a factory—a "notions" factory, which was then engaged in adding to the beauty of the world by manufacturing colored and embossed tin-lids; later it made fancy brass buttons and can-openers. *"Et comme il était très fort, hardi, courageux et avisé"*—he soon obtained, not like St. Julian the Hospitalier, the command of a battalion—but a wage sufficient to let him save money. They saved money, he and his missus, and after eight years, they built themselves a frame house—"a proper, warm 'aouse for them frosty winters and we had one of those 'ere proper iron stoves. Proper!"

On the first morning of the new house—I presume his missus had lit the proper stove—he was jest a-puttin' on his collar, when he heard a crackling. He thought it was the frost in the apple trees, cracking the boughs. But, in forty minutes the house was gone.

He had meant to insure that afternoon. So he and his missus—he never described her, but I think she must have been a gallant soul—aged fifty-six a-piece, went back to boarding-house life and work in the "notion" factory. Next autumn, coming back from work one evening, he noticed in a neighbor's lot, a fine apple tree. Proper, with apples on it, these 'ere large codlins! He offered the neighbor two dollars for the apples on the tree and peddled them round the town.

In five years, at that trade, he had made enough to think of "retiring". Then he see in the pipers that Hengland needed men. So he ses to his missus: "We've got money enough to do as we please. Let's go and see what we can do to 'elp the ol' gal. . . ." As if Victoria had been still on the throne. They came to London, and he went to see the ol' firm. His sons said to him:

No, they were married men with families. "So I says to the missus: 'I ain't got no family, I ain't.' " And he bought her an 'aouse at 'Endon and an annuity, through the ol' firm. That had taken till February, 1916. He was apologetic over the delay, but he had wanted to see the ol' woman settled comfortable.

February, 1916—it was then July. Thirteen weeks training, you see, and he had been two months in France, "mostly on this 'ere ol' Somme." He was sixty-one years and four months of age. And he said he felt tired.

There was about his narration nothing of the "narquois" humor of the cockney; but, colorlessly, as tired farm-laborers talk, he went on talking—as if it was just the Will of God. I met some of his officers a couple of weeks later and asked about him, but his story grew rather hazy. They found a Company Sergeant-Major who said he had thought the old man was a bit too old for his job in the trenches. I daresay the old man had found rough gentlenesses and kindly helping hands from his mate and the noncommissioned officers of his battalion. He would have, of course. So the C.S.M. had detailed him for caretaker at the baths. The old man had enlisted as being thirty years and six months of age—just half his years. The C.S.M. remembered that; but he didn't know what had become of the man. He rather thought he had been killed on the 24/7/'16 by a shell pitched in the battle, but perhaps he hadn't.

It was mostly his tired voice and his colorless narration that had impressed me with him. I didn't think much about—I did not even realize—the rather stupendous Odyssey of a life he must have had until I stood on that balcony of the Paris theater, in the night, with the French officers. You see, it was anyhow such a tremendous Odyssey for every one there that a little more or less at the moment did not jump to the eye as mattering. But, underneath, in the subconscious mind, it mattered.

I daresay—nay, I am sure—that it was that quality that mattered to me more than anything else of the whole cause for thought that the war gave one. For me—apart from Lord Kitchener and Sir Edward Grey—there were few great figures of those years. Sir Edward Grey went out of course once war was declared: then Kitchener went. There remained this Tommy of the Lincolns and I think Lt. Morgan of my own battalion was then still alive. Henri Gaudier was certainly dead—and he, in my mind, was united to the Lincolnshire Private and Morgan. They had, all three, a certain serenity.

I wish I could remember Morgan's initials. He had a brother, "I. H."—a nice boy. I hope he is still alive.

But the Morgan who is dead sounded, as it were, exactly the same note as the Lincolnshire man—the note of tired but continuous laboring after a very hard life. You know the sort of effect a violin has when its strings are muted. It was like that.

I think Morgan must have had his last leave at the same time as myself when I went out the second time; but I don't think we went out together. At any rate, we took together a very long railway journey—but I don't remember why or where—probably because I spent it listening to the story of his life. I remember his tired movements as he took his knapsack down from the rack whilst the train was running into some terminus. And I remember it seemed to me to be a shame—on the part of destiny—that he should be going out at all. I met him next night in Coventry Street—and he did not seem to be getting much out of Coventry Street after dark. We stood talking for a minute, and then he disappeared among the prostitutes and the flash Jews. I expect we each said: "Good luck, old man," for I believe he liked me, and I must have liked him very much.

He was killed, as I have said, by a *minenwerfer* as he was going up a communication-trench on his first night. He was buried so that, in the morning when they found him, only his feet and legs were showing. He was probably not buried alive, because the officer who found him said that he was smiling. I like to think of that.

Because these were the men who needed—who *must* have had if indeed there be a just God or even merely a deity who gives compensations—a period of sanctuary after their very hard labors. It doesn't matter about you and me. . . .

But poor old Morgan . . . I don't know what age he was. I daresay he was no more than thirty-two, little and brown and persistent—his face was thin, aquiline, and as if hardened and sand-blasted by the perpetual confrontation of winds full of hail. For he too had gone out to Canada—but as a boy, apparently without much capital, to work for wheat-farmers.

I suppose most people know something about working for Canadian farmers—the long solitudes, the distance of the towns, the protracted buggy rides over immense plains. Well, I seem to have an extraordinary sense of it—just from the way Morgan talked on that long train journey. I don't know that I remember incidents. Perhaps I could. I remember that, knowing little about horses at the beginning, he was asked by the boss if he would take a helluva vicious team to the nearest township to fetch something, a plow, I think. And he had done it.

But the main of the story was just the long strain—long hours merging into long years, with the muscles always a little overstrained. Not much, but a little. Because, though gallant, persistent, and showing it as the Welsh do, he was small for wrestling with tree trunks and immense plains. I remember his saying that when he had dug holes for the posts of wire fencing, he poured water in so that the posts should freeze solid in their places.

Well, he too must have been *"hardi, courageux, et avisé"*—leading a long, uncolored life of sober chastity, without many visits to the townships even, let alone the towns. For, as he sat in the carriage, he said that he owned property—timber lots and other lots, bought out of the savings of a laborer.

And he spoke of going back there, *après la guerre finie*—with the serene resignation of a man with no other imaginable destiny before him. It was to be more toil and more toil and more toil. He did not, apparently, ask for—certainly he did not imagine—any other future. So that resignation is not the right word. Serenity is. . . .

X

From a Balcony

One of the French officers, on the balcony of the theater, during the *entr'acte* of *Lakme,* was describing, with that depressed neatness of quiet diction that is at the disposal of every educated Frenchman, the sleep of a French territorial on an uncompleted traverse. The others had, as it were—and as if by preconcertion—capped stories in lauding and pitying the *territoriaux*. These troops, it may be as well to point out, were something like the Labor Battalions that subsequently we raised. I fancy we had nothing of the sort at that date and indeed, between Hélie and Corbie I had lately seen the Guards' Brigade doing fatigue that, in French-France would have been performed by old fathers and grandfathers. That, of course, is nothing to the discredit of that great brigade. As soon as battalions, brigades, or divisions came out of the trenches for a "rest", they were given the cheerful jobs of repairing rear-line trenches, digging drains, cleaning out latrines, and the like. When we came out from the Somme for a "month's rest", first A Company, then B, C, and D were given an all-night fatigue—of mending the Albert-Amiens road! And in August! Then we were moved up into the salient.

At any rate, slowly, coldly, and without the shadow of a shade of cordiality, in the blackness of the Paris night, the French officers piled it up. We were not popular in France at that date, and I don't know that, except as individuals, we deserved popularity. That does not matter. The fact remained that they were "out" to make one feel that from under every little cowering roof in France, from Orange as from the frontier by Mentone to the other frontier by Longwy, old, stiff men, with horny hands and faded eyes had marched over the endless roads with the poplars to their too-heavy labors amidst the bursting shells. . . . From under *every* cowering roof of every township, town, hamlet, and parish; from every *arrondissement;* from every *subprefecture;* from every *departement.* Coldly, like inquisitors, in the darkness, they let me have that information. It was not really necessary. I knew it already. But I was too tired, harassed, dispirited to tell them so. I, too, was old for that job. *Atque ego. . . .*

For I couldn't get away from the conviction that they were talking at me with a purpose—that they were, in indirect terms, telling me that it was a scandal that the Brigade of Guards should be employed in clearing out latrines, work which, in French-France, was performed by the fathers and the grandfathers—the guards being tired out and worn down by such employment when they were such splendid fighting material and should have been really rested. I daresay our own war office would have answered that that was part of our discipline and that "fatigues" when men were "resting" were good for their livers and kept them "fit". There is such a school of thought. Anyhow, I am not writing a military treatise and do not ask that any attention should be paid to my views. I am only chronicling the psychology of an Infantry officer as he was affected by certain circumstances.

And I *couldn't* get away from the conviction that the French officers were talking "officially". In those days there had just been published in Paris a book of "official" propaganda by myself. It would not have been a different book if it had been unofficial or if there had been no war. It simply advanced the theory that in the world of letters and ideas, for personal industry and pride in work as work, it is only France that matters among the nations. I had said that when I was twenty; I resaid it then being over double that age; I resay it today; and I will resay it as my eyes close in death. No one in my country has ever paid any attention to one's saying it, and no one ever will. Why should they? Letters and ideas have so little place in our body politic and the doctrine of pride in work as work; of engrossment and of serenity; of aloofness from the world and of introspection with no other purpose—is here anathema both with the Right which hates the doctrine of Art for Art's sake and with the Left, which hates that of Labor for the sake of Labor. Yet I see no other lesson in life. That is why I have collected these notes upon sheepfolds—this long lay sermon.

So this particular piece of official propaganda was, just then, being accorded an extraordinary amount of notoriety in France. The skill of our own propaganda people and the patriotism of distinguished Frenchmen accounted for that. It was reviewed at enormous length and with enormous headlines by Academicians, by assailants of the French Academy, and by the Mayors of Rouen, Lyons, and Toulouse. It was "communicated" to the Institute of France; publicly laid upon the shelves of the city library of Yvetot. And it was no doubt on that account that the French officers presented official views to me so carefully and so excruciatingly. They imagined that I had weight in the Councils of the Empire, as would have been the case in their own country.

While they talked the black houses round the market had infinite depths of violet against the white stars. But all the same I was looking at the view from the top of the great brick Roman Theater at Orange—over the flats with the ragged, stunted vines, the stubble, and the thatched roofs. Yes, I knew that beside Orange the little houses cowered beside the furrows and that on the other frontier great, gaunt piles were subsiding under scrolls and tongues of flame, going down to a last rest as the very tired men of a platoon will fall out beside the road. And the great buildings never get up again.

For I never feel that houses have souls. So that, when, out there, you saw a house go down as fire, it seemed to do it luxuriously almost. It was finished with men and their ways. It had no doubt borne for long with their cruelties, stupidities, imbecilities; with its windows for mournful eyes it had seen the generations flit past and fade. It had known cold that made its timbers crack and the great heat of the sun warping them. But beneath the flames, slowly, it would sink to the earth from which it had come. Yes, luxuriously, as men stretch themselves down for a long rest. . . .

The French officer was still talking about the old territorial who had fallen asleep. It seems that the old man had gone on working, after his mates had been taken off for a spell, on the inner face of the traverse —which is a sort of pillar of earth with a gangway round it, left in a trench to minimize the lateral spread of shell fire. He had gone on working—out of pure zeal, the officer said. The officer addressed me with hard bitterness. I suppose he thought I was some sort of noncombatant. The staff-captain told me afterward that this officer, being aide-de-camp to one of the most famous French generals of division of the day had, the night before, attended his chief to a dinner—given, I think, by the British A.P.M.—in the course of which the heroic doings of a great many British Regiments were extolled. And then, in a pause, an English lady had said to the French general: "And the French haven't done so badly." . . . I was being made to suffer for this.

And I did suffer a good deal—more I think than I ever suffered. The officer went on and on about his old territorial. He was there, asleep, in the light of a single candle stuck in the clay. He was as it were spread-eagled against the earth. His legs apart he had raised his hammer to strike his chisel; both his arms were over his head, stretched out. And he was just asleep. It was touching; it was terrible in its simplicity, the officer said. He said the territorial came from Passy—as it might be Putney.

It was just at this point that I remembered Morgan and the old man of the bath-mill. I daresay you will think it merely a literary trick, when I say that I saw them.

But I *saw* them: against an immense black mass fringed by flaming houses. I saw those two, tired faces; the two serene, honest, and simple souls, who had the Kingdom of God within them. And it seemed to me that they had died in vain.

It was for me the most terrible moment of the war.

I daresay that for many people it was the most horrible period of the war. For, by then it had become apparent that the Somme advance was a fiasco—a useless butchery. We knew we should never advance. I daresay the French knew it better than we. Certainly the voices of these officers drove it home: they spoke as if they were talking to a condemned criminal. And I think it was not right of them.

We, at any rate, were the old voluntary army. We had come, aged or young, from the ends of the earth. I don't know whether it is worse to be old or young in a great war—it was bad enough to be old! And I don't know whether it was better or worse to have come from the ends of the earth—or from Passy. Or to have passed all one's life beneath a roof that shuddered with fear. . . . If you had done that, you were more used to the idea, and to the discipline of the idea, of war. You discussed the moves, here and there, more *en connoisseur*.

But I doubt if one of those men on the balcony felt the war as I did. We, after all, brought so many more emotions to it. You had only to contrast Paris, gray, sober, much as usual, with the roads under leisurely repair, and the old horses and the old *cochers* and *voitures* dawdling in the shadow of the plane-trees—

with London, plastered with endless appeals in blue and scarlet and yellow—London, hurrying, exclaiming, clamoring. . . . The old territorial had lived all his life under the shadow—and it came. The old private of the Lincolnshires had never thought of such an end. But it came! And Europe flamed. . . .

And the worst of it all was that one was beginning to doubt. Until then one had been carried by the fine wave of enthusiasm. It seemed to embrace the whole country. And we in all the holes, valleys, over all the downlands of the Somme, where the sun shone with its chalky rays as it does by L——, had had a great singleness of purpose and had been confident that we had the support of a great singleness of purpose extending across a world. But doubt had begun to creep in. . . .

I wished, then, that I had not read "What Maisie Knew" in the bath at Albert. I wished that the daily papers would not reach us. The atmosphere shown so overwhelmingly in the book was beginning to be too close to the atmosphere reflected in the papers. And we were, truly, very lonely out there; truly we were some millions of men, suspended on a raft, in limitless space.

And we were beginning to feel a curious dislike of the civilians whom up till then we had so trusted —a curious dislike that was never to die. I don't know what was going on at home: political intrigues no doubt; strikes possibly. But there seemed to prevail a tenuous, misty struggle of schemes—just the atmosphere of "Maisie." I don't think that many of those who were one's comrades *in illo die* did not at times feel a certain hopelessness. It was as if at times we said: What are those people after? Aren't they—aren't they surely?—"out" to make huge profits from our poor Tommies; to cut down the rations of our poor Tommies; and to gain notoriety by forcing on a timorous central government their own schemes for the training of poor Tommies—schemes that have resulted in the deaths of hundreds of thousands of our poor fine Tommies? And, when their own attractions were enhanced by the bringing off of this or that scheme, intrigue, or cabal, they would vote to themselves ribbons, orders, power, divorces, and the right to gallons of petrol. And so they would sit in the chairs of the lost and the forgotten amidst a world where the ideals which sent all those millions to destruction were lost too . . . and forgotten. You will say that this is bitter. It is. It was bitter to have seen the 38th Division murdered in Mametz Wood—and to guess what underlay that! . . .

And then the French officer said what I knew he would say: what I had known that, with all his cold lack of rhetoric, he was working up to. He said that the old, sleeping territorial looked like Our Lord on Calvary. I could have screamed. Upon my soul I could have screamed. And, if I hadn't thought it just possible that his dislike attached to me personally, I daresay I should have talked to him as I talked to the other French officer as the reader may see in *Une Partie de Cricket.* But the faint hope that it was just myself that he despised and not poor Morgan and the others—all the poor others along that long front of ours—that faint hope that he was attacking only me and not the Army of the Somme just made me hold my peace until we went back into the theater. And in the theater I suddenly remembered—as clearly as I had remembered the others—Henri Gaudier. He, too, seemed to stand before me and to smile at me a little, as if he found me comic. . . .

I do not know why it is that now, when I think of Gaudier, the cadence that I hear in my mind should be one of sadness. For there was never any one further from sadness than Henri Gaudier, whether in his being or in his fate. He had youth; he had grace of person and of physique; he had a sense of the comic. He had friendships, associates in his work, loves, the hardships that help youth. He had genius, and he died a hero.

He comes back to me best as he was at a function of which I remember most, except for Gaudier, disagreeable sensations—embarrassments. It was an "affair"—one of two—financed by a disagreeably obese Neutral whom I much disliked. That would be in late July, 1914. The Neutral was much concerned to get out of a country and a city which appeared to be in danger. Some one else—several some ones—were intensely anxious, each of them, to get money out of the very fat, very monied, disagreeably intelligent being. And I was ordered, by *Les Jeunes,* to be there. It was a parade, in fact. I suppose that even then I was regarded as a, I hope benevolent, grandfather, by a number of members of an advanced school.[1] Anyhow, that comes back

[1] For the benefit of the uninstructed reader, I may say that new Schools of Art, like new commercial enterprises, need both backers with purses and backers of a certain solid personal appearance or weight in the world. And it is sometimes disagreeable, though it is always a duty, to be such an individual.

to me as a disagreeable occasion of evil passions, evil people, of bad, flashy cooking in an underground haunt of pre-war smartness.

I daresay it was not really as bad as all that—but when I am forced to receive the hospitality of persons whom I dislike, the food seems to go bad, and there is a bad taste in the mouth, symbol of a disturbed liver. So the band played in that cave and the head ached and there were nasty foreign waiters and bad, very expensive, champagne.

There were also speeches—and one could not help knowing that the speeches were directed at the Neutral's breeches pockets. The Neutral leaned heavily sideways at table, devouring the bad food at once with gluttony and nonchalance. It talked about its motor car, which apparently was at Liverpool or Southampton—somewhere where there were liners, quays, cordage, cranes; all ready to abandon a city which would be doomed should Armageddon become Armageddon. The speeches went on. . . .

Then Gaudier rose. It was suddenly like a silence that intervened during a distressing and ceaseless noise. I don't know that I had ever noticed him before except as one amongst a crowd of dirtyish, bearded, slouch-hatted individuals, like conspirators; but, there, he seemed as if he stood amidst sunlight; as if indeed he floated in a ray of sunlight, like the dove in Early Italian pictures. In a life during which I have known thousands of people; thousands and thousands of people; during which I have grown sick and tired of "people" so that I prefer the society of cabbages, goats, and the flowers of the marrow plant; I have never otherwise known what it was to witness an appearance which symbolized so completely—aloofness. It was like the appearance of Apollo at a creditors' meeting. It was supernatural.

It was just that. One didn't rub one's eyes: one was too astounded. Only, something within one wondered what the devil he was doing there. If he hadn't seemed so extraordinarily efficient, one would have thought he had strayed, from another age, from another world, from some Hesperides. One keeps wanting to say that he was Greek, but he wasn't. He wasn't of a type that strayed: and indeed I seem to feel his poor bones moving in the August dust of Neuville St. Vaast when I—though even only nearly!—apply to him a name that he would have hated. At any rate, it was amazing to see him there; since he seemed so entirely inspired by inward visions that one wondered what he could be after—certainly not the bad dinner, the attentions of the foreign waiters, a try at the Neutral's money-bag strings. No, he spoke as if his eyes were fixed on a point within himself; and yet, with such humor and such good-humor—as if he found the whole thing so comic!

One is glad of the comic in his career; it would otherwise have been too much an incident of the Elgin marble type. But even the heroism of his first, abortive "joining up" was heroico-comic. As I heard him tell the story, or at least as I remember it, it was like this:

He had gone to France in the early days of the war —and one accepted his having gone as one accepted the closing of a door—of a tomb, if you like. Then, suddenly, he was once more there. It produced a queer effect; it was a little bewildering in a bewildering world. But it became comic. He had gone to Boulogne and presented himself to the Recruiting Officer—an N. C. O., or captain, of the old school, white moustachios, *cheveux en brosse*. Gaudier stated that he had left France without having performed his military duties, but, since *la patrie* was in danger, he had returned like any other good little *piou-piou.* But the sergeant, martinet-wise, as became a veteran of 1870, struck the table with his fist and exclaimed:

"*Non, mon ami,* it is not *la patrie,* but you who are in danger. You are a deserter; you will be shot." So Gaudier was conducted to a motor, in which, under the military escort of two files of men, a sergeant, a corporal, and a lieutenant, he was whirled off to Calais. In Calais Town he was placed in an empty room. Outside the door were stationed two men with large guns, and Gaudier was told that, if he opened the door, the guns would go off. That was his phrase. He did not open the door. He spent several hours reflecting that though they manage these things better in France, they don't manage them so damn well. At the end of that time he pushed aside the window blind and looked out. The room was on the ground floor; there were no bars. Gaudier opened the window; stepped into the street, just like that—and walked back to Boulogne.

He returned to London.

He was drawn back again to France by the opening of the bombardment of Rheims Cathedral. This time he had a safe conduct from the Embassy. I do not know the date of his second joining up or the number of his regiment. At any rate, he took part in an attack on a Prussian outpost on Michaelmas Eve, so he had not much delayed, and his regiment was rendered illustrious, though it cannot have given him a deuce of a lot of training. He did not need it. He was as hard as nails and as intelligent as the devil. He was used to forging and grinding his own chisels. He was inured to the hardships of poverty in great cities; he was accustomed to hammer and chisel at his marble for hours and hours of day after day. He was a "fit" townsman—and it was "fit" townsmen who conducted the fighting of 1914 when the war was won: it was *les parigots*.

Of his biography I have always had only the haziest of notions. I know that he was the son of a Meridional craftsman, a carpenter and joiner, who was a good workman and no man could have a better. His father was called Joseph Gaudier—so why he called himself B'jesker, I do not know. I prefer really to be hazy; because Gaudier will always remain for me something supernatural. He was for me a "message" at a difficult time of life. His death and the death at the same time of another boy—but quite a commonplace, nice boy—made a rather doubtful way quite plain to me.

All my life I have been very much influenced by a Chinese proverb—to the effect that it would be hypocrisy to seek for the person of the Sacred Emperor in a low teahouse. It is a bad proverb, because it is so wise and so enervating. It has "ruined my career".

When, for instance, I founded a certain Review, losing, for me, immense sums of money on it, or when the contributors unanimously proclaimed that I had not paid them for their contributions—which was not true because they certainly had among them a quantity of my money in their pockets—or when a suffrage bill failed to pass in the Commons; or when some one's really good book has not been well reviewed; or when I have been robbed, slandered, or abortively blackmailed—in all the vicissitudes of life, misquoted on it, I have always first shrugged my shoulders and murmured that it would be hypocrisy to seek for the person of the Sacred Emperor in a low tea-shop. It meant that it would be hypocrisy to expect a taste for the finer letters in a large public's discernment in critics; honesty in aesthetes or literati; public spirit in lawgivers; accuracy in pundits; gratitude in those one has saved from beggary, and so on.

So, when I first noticed Henri Gaudier—which was in an underground restaurant, the worst type of thieves' kitchen—these words rose to my lips. I did not, you understand, believe that he would exist and be so wise, so old, so gentle, so humorous, such a genius. I did not really believe that he had shaved, washed, assumed garments that fitted his great personal beauty.

For he had great personal beauty. If you looked at him casually, you imagined that you were looking at one of those dock-rats of the Marseilles quays, who will carry your baggage for you, pimp for you; garotte you and throw your body overboard—but who will do it all with an air, an ease, an exquisiteness of manners! They have, you see, the traditions and inherited knowledge of such ancient nations in Marseilles—of Etruscans, Phoenicians, Colonial Greeks, Late Romans, Troubadours, Late French—and that of those who first sang the Marseillaise! And many of them, whilst they are young, have the amazing beauty that Gaudier had. Later, absinthe spoils it—but for the time, they are like Arlésiennes.

All those wisdoms, then, looked out of the eyes of

Gaudier—and God only knows to what he threw back —to Etruscans or Phoenicians, no doubt, certainly not to the Greeks who colonized Marseilles, or the Late Romans who succeeded to them. He seemed, then, to have those wisdoms behind his eyes somewhere. And he had, certainly, an astounding erudition.

I don't know where he picked it up—but his conversation was overwhelming—and his little history of sculpture by itself will give you more flashes of inspiration than you will ever, otherwise, gather from the whole of your life. His sculpture itself affected me just as he did.

In odd places—the sitting rooms of untidy and eccentric poets with no particular merits, in appalling exhibitions, in nasty night clubs, in dirty restaurants one would be stopped for a moment in the course of a sentence by the glimpse of a brutal chunk of rock that seemed to have lately fallen unwanted from a slate quarry, or, in the alternative, by a little piece of marble that seemed to have the tightened softness of the haunches of a fawn—of some young creature of the underwoods, an ancient, shyly-peopled, thicket.

The brutalities would be the work of Mr. Epstein—

the other, Gaudier. For Gaudier's work had just his own, personal, impossible quality. And one did not pay much attention to it simply because one did not believe in it. It was too good to be true. Remembering the extraordinary rush that the season of 1914 was, it appears a miserable tragedy, but it is not astonishing, that one's subliminal mind should whisper to me, every time we caught that glimpse of a line: "It is hypocrisy to search for the person of the Sacred Emperor in a low tea-house." It was of course the devil who whispered that. So I never got the sensation I might have got from that line. Because one did not believe in that line. One thought: "It is just the angle at which one's chair in the restaurant presents to one an accidental surface of one of these young men's backs."

And then a day came when there was no doubt about it. Gaudier was a Lance Corporal in the 4th Section, 7th Company, 129th Regt. of Infantry of the Line.[1] Gaudier was given his three stripes for "gallantry in face of the enemy". One read in a letter:

"I am at rest for three weeks in a village, that is, I

[1] The knowledgeable reader will observe that here Gringoire has consulted the monograph on Gaudier by Mr. Pound—the best piece of craftsmanship that Mr. Pound has put together; or at least the best this writer has read of that author's.

am undergoing a course of study to be promoted officer when necessary during an offensive."

Or in another letter:

"I imagine a dull dawn, two lines of trenches, and in between explosion on explosion with clouds of black and yellow smoke, a ceaseless noise from the rifles, a few legs and heads flying, and me standing up among all this like to Mephisto—commanding: *'Feu par salves à 250 mètres—joue—feu!'*

"Today is magnificent, a fresh wind, clear sun, and larks singing cheerfully. . . ."

That was it!

But just because it was so commonplace; so sordid, so within the scope of all our experiences, powers of observation, and recording, it all seemed impossible to believe that in *that* particular low tea-house there were really Youth, Beauty, Erudition, Fortune, Genius—to believe in the existence of a Gaudier! The devil still whispered to me: "That would be hypocrisy!" For if you would not believe that genius could show itself during the season of 1914, how *could* you believe that, of itself, inscrutable, noiseless, it would go out of our discreditable world where the literati and the æsthetes were sweating, harder than they ever, ever did after *le mot juste* or the Line of Beauty, to find excuses that should keep them from the trenches—that, so quietly, the greatest genius of them all would go into that world of misery.

And then I read:

"Mort pour la patrie.

"After ten months of fighting and two promotions for gallantry, on the field, Henri Gaudier-Brzeska, in a charge at Neuville St. Vaast. June 5, 1915."

Alas, when it was too late, I had learned that, to this low tea-shop that the world is, from time to time the Sacred Emperor may pay visits. So I began to want to kill certain people. I still do—for the sake of Gaudier and those few who are like him.

For the effect of reading that announcement was to make me remember with extraordinary vividness a whole crowd of the outlines of pieces of marble, of drawings, of tense and delicate lines at which, in the low tea-house of the year before's season, I had only nonchalantly glanced. The Sacred Emperor, then, had been there. He seemed, at last, to be an extraordinarily real figure—as real as one of the other sculptor's brutal chunks of granite. Only, because of the crowd one hadn't seen him—the crowd of blackmailers,[1] sneak-thieves, suborners, pimps, reviewers, and the commonplace and the indifferent—the Huns of London. Well, it became—and it still more remains! one's duty to try to kill them. There are probably several Sacred Emperors still at large—though the best of them will have been killed, as Gaudier was.

It was whilst I was inside the theater that I registered, as the saying is, a mental vow that I would pay no attention any more to public affairs. To do so would drive one mad. I decided that I must put my head down under the cloth for the rest of the war. And I think I did so. Except for the occasional duty of writing propaganda—which from that time onwards I did in French—I paid no more attention to the politics of my country or the world. I just did the collar-work of the Infantry Officer until the 11/11/'17. After

[1] Gringoire is too fond of this word—which he uses in a special sense to indicate persons—mostly reviewers—who do not appreciate the work of himself and his school. In his conversation he introduced at this point a long denunciation of the —— Literary Supplement, principally because, whilst purporting to be a literary paper, it devotes, according to him, 112/113ths of its space to books about facts, at the expense of works of the imagination. So he calls that respectable journal a blackmailing organ. Since, however, this is a topic that can hardly interest the non-literary, and since the literary are hardly likely to read these pages, the compiler has taken the liberty of not reporting these sallies. It may be true that Pontius Pilate is more criminal than the crucified thieves—but it is *never* politic to say so.

that, my views being too favorable to France, the Ministry of Information and the censor suppressed or lost in the post my rather excited writings on the Terms of Peace. . . . That would be about three years ago today. It seems a long while. . . .

The inside of the theater was brilliant, formal, a little shabby if you looked closely. Of the performance of *Lakme*—an opera that I love very much, since the music is soft, moving, and generous—I remember very little. So it must have been a good rendering with no performer in particular "sticking out". The British naval officers were rather funny. And I think it is no left-handed compliment to the composer, Délibes—though it may be to the librettist—to say that my thoughts were elsewhere. The music was just sensuous pleasure; the aspect of the house, spreading round in great lines of polychromatic humanity, more regular than is the case with most theaters in London—more suave and more classical—soothed one after what was certainly an emotional crisis; an escaped danger. For it would have mortified me for the rest of my life if I had burst out under the goadings of the French officers. But, by the Grace of God and the skin of my teeth, I had retained, quite certainly, my aspect of insular phlegm.

Still it had been exhausting—and I was enervated. And then, quite suddenly, it came to me to wonder what was going on outside the theater—what was going on under the black roof of the night, with the infinitely numerous population of leaves, blades, branches, reeds beside streams, great trees in the woodlands—and with the silent, watchful population of the thickets where the shadows are so extremely deep. I found myself wondering what time of year it was. And I said: the first weeks of September. For that morning I had recollected that, two years before on that day, the Germans had turned back from in front of Paris. Forty-six years before they had won the battle of Sedan.

It was, then, during the first weeks of September. But what happened—in September? One forgot. One had repaired trenches; one had commanded fatigues digging drains round Bn.H.Q., to the left of Mount Kemmel. One had dug so efficiently that, during the first thunderstorm the repaired trenches below were neck-deep in water. All that had passed in "the Country".

But what happened in September? There were no doubt apples on the trees, and, certainly, it was the time of year when many cobwebs, frail nets across the tall grasses on commons or single, brilliant filaments, streamed out and glistened on still, bright days.

There would be plums, too; but what about damsons? Wasn't it early for them? And how about garden peas? Were they over? And field peas? And would there be an autumn feel in the air?

It was twenty-one days to Michaelmas—and Michaelmas certainly brought the autumn feeling, with touches of vine in the shadow of yellowing plants and the leaves of sunflowers drooping straight down, like unfurled colors on windless days. But in copses, shaves, and spinneys were the leaves on forest trees yet turning? Were roads yet hard and frosty in the morning? And were horses yet sluggish and apt to stumble on roads as they do at the turn of the year and the fall of the leaf? . . . Time to give 'em a ball.

The baffled mind seemed to stumble at all these questions. One was in the theater and having been forbidden by the will to think that what surrounded the great walls with their human lining was a vast black map fringed by conflagrations, the poor mind hung faltering.

It fell suddenly back on contemplating the green nook that—on the down behind Albert—it had reserved for itself. Yes, the mind actually did that. And, across the gilding of the proscenium, across Lakme's singing the great song of yearning, there hung a slight shimmer of green that intensified itself and took shape like a recumbent oval. . . . And there began to become visible the yellowing, grayish rows of broad beans; a rather ragged hedge and a little stream beyond, level with the grass and fringed with the glistening stems of clumps of rushes that had been cut for thatching stacks. Because it was indeed September.

XI

"Rosalie Prudent"

ONE evening the compiler addressed Gringoire, who was making notes in a seed catalogue, somewhat as follows:

"Do you remember, oh Gringoire, what it is to awake of a September morning at dawn? Being *horticulteur,* your first thought will be for the weather: being *poète,* your first thought will be for your new volume. And the two first thoughts will overlay the one the other, according as chance wills. But the still mist is so reassuring as to the weather that you can put that aside and think only of your volume. The goodly fruits of the earth in the late summer season, the plums, the apples, the quinces; the maize, the marrows, the melons, have yet another day, for sure, of bright, warm sun, of gorgeous, mellow downward shavers of sun. They, surely, shall stand motionless in the warmth.

"But the poems . . . oh my poor Gringoire of the

dawn: the great, half-finished epic! Ah that! that seemed so glowing too when last night in the golden light of the two candles, in your poor little, rickety salon that yet has a style of its own . . . you read them to Madame Sélysette . . . the poor verses that you read so famously to little Madame! . . . In the dawn, ah, the wolf of the night that says: 'Hou . . . hou' from the mountains has not gone home! Almost you hear his sniffing round the little green door that, because yours is a land of idylls and the innocent, you have left open. One day the wolf with the great, cocked hairy ears, with the long white teeth like razors for their sharpness shall come in. You will hear upon the uncarpeted stairway the pad of the feet; the little thin door will push open, and raised at the foot of your small white bed, you will see the great beast; the huge head; the bloodshot eyes. . . . And Madame, in the other little white bed across the small white room will moan a little in her sleep. . . .

"All the poor verses: the little lines! How shall they be the barbed wire fence that shall keep the wolf from the door of the cottage? Why, he could push the poor, tindery old walls down with his snout! The poor verses! They halt . . . or no, they do not halt. We are too good a craftsman for that! But assuredly they do not run. And the publisher! What shall he say? And Madame with such a need of a new gown: it should have been of velvet, puffed in the arms, and slashed to show an undercoat of crushed rose silk. And to tell the truth—your *pantalons?* How they shine in the seat, like a mirror! And the public! Ah, the grim public that has no taste but for dominoes in the cafés of an evening! How shall they care for the savor of lavender and rosemary in your smaller verses? What, to them, are Melpomene and Mélisande and Maleine and Musidore of your epic! And the cursed 'machinery' of the enormous poem! What has become of your great device that was to take the story forward from line 1100 to line 1424? Forgotten! O Apollo! O Euterpe! Forgotten—gone—your brain is failing. Your diet of oatmeal and junket is not enough to water your gray matter with rich red blood. It is all over . . . and the great wolf says 'Hou! . . . hou!' upon the mountains, though the mists are rising. And Madame, you can see, is smiling in her sleep! Ah! When you are suspended by your cravat from the old thorn tree, she will marry the rich son of the apothecary. . . .

"And then . . . suddenly you remember! Maleine

became a rose tree, and the slipper of glass was hidden in a bath. . . . Yes: it was like that. The device has come back to you. Hurray! Hurray! And the verses shall glow and sparkle. And damn the public and damn and damn the publisher, and Madame is a sweet, plump angel.

"And you spring from your bed, oh Gringoire, but with the footfall of a panther for fear the creaking of the very old oak floor boards should awaken your own Sélysette. And quick and quick to your dressing room, which is on state occasions the spare bedroom. Then you wash in the brick-floored kitchen. And how crisp and reviving is the cold water on the skin—just as it used to be when you came out of the tent or the dugout or the hut, down before Péronne in the old days. And there is no war.

"No war to awaken the birds that are still sleeping in the massed shadows of trees all unmoving in the deep mists. A noble, long, quiet, warm day of September is before you. A day of *moissons* and *vendanges,* ripening securely, still; with line added to line in the morning; and nothing to do in that rich little garden of yours; and line added to line of the epic all the afternoon. And a stroll in the level, sinking rays of the sun with Madame Sélysette, like a mysterious *jeune fille* once more, to sing to you, in the carefreedom of her heart, the song of the raggle-taggle gipsies, oh. . . .

> 'Oh what care I for my goose-feather-bed
> The sheets turned down so bravely oh!
> Tonight I'll sleep on a cold open heath
> Along with the raggle-taggle gipsies, oh!'

as she was used to sing it in the days when she left the roof of her father, the so very rich goldsmith of Toulouse, to take up with you, oh my so very poor poet. *Vogue la galère!* I hear you say. For are there not fine cabbages in the garden; and the haricots and the tomatoes all a-ripening! And does not Madame make an incomparable *potage bonne femme* with these things and a few little bones! A fig for the wolf! And if she cannot have her gown of velvet—when do her dark eyes sparkle more vivaciously than when in her black hair she wears a coronal of the scarlet berries of bryony? And if the *pantalons* shine in the seat, let them shine till they wear through! And then there will be a piece of sacking to insert, whose remainder shall stuff up the holes of the so very old roof. And Melpomene and Mélisande and Musidore shall dance to the tune of green sleeves round the rose tree that was Maleine! Aye, they shall dance in the sun till the crystal slipper falls out of the bath of dew. And already Phœbus Apollo has chased into the farthest recesses of the Alpilles the craven old wolf. . . .

"And, fastening your collar, you rush into the room where Madame is asleep, and you shout out:

" 'I have it! We will put Sweet Williams, and behind them Canterbury Bells, and behind them Hollyhocks, in the bed along the path. And tulips before the door!'

"It is true that the Hollyhocks will then be to the south of the Canterbury Bells, and they again to the south of the Sweet Williams—the tall plants standing in the light of the short ones, which is against the maxims of safe gardeners. But we must chance something, as we chance life when we are so very poor and so very simple and have to adventure down the years with no stores of gold, under a very old roof with half the tiles off. And besides: maybe next summer will be a very dry summer, and then the shade of the Hollyhock on the Canterbury Bells, and of the Canterbury Bells on the Sweet Williams will be a positive benefit. . . .

"And, truly, in all the gardening year—which is all pleasure except for such lets and hindrances as God decrees to you in order that you may remember that you are human—there is no pleasure to equal the pleasures of a mid-September day. For there is promise in the chrysanthemums; the asters, petunias, and geraniums are still bright; marrows, pumpkins, gourds, maize, plums, apples, pears, damsons are drinking in the sun and turning all the colors from rich green to orange and tomato-scarlet. There are still flowers on the roses and on the sweet-pea hedge. And, if those foliages are thinning, through their silver and yellow haze you can see the bright mosaic of next summer's beds! Ah, brave mid-September!"

To this Gringoire answered—a little grimly:

In a mid-September twilight, the rain poured down on Pont-de-Nieppe. Depressed Highlanders lounged along the street in front of the row of villas that ran from the church to the rear of the town—taking our own lines as the front. One's horse and one's orderly's horse slipped disagreeably on the wet granite setts of the pavé, and one seemed to have gone backwards and forwards, in a deluge over greasy roads for hours and hours—for a whole lifetime. One seemed never to have done anything else. It was a billeting job that we had been sent upon. And, when we had billeted everything we could think of, there still remained some disreputable other ranks connected with the divisional canteen, for whom we had not found holes, corners, and a shop. And the division we were relieving had apparently vanished and so had the Town Marshal, whilst the *Maire* was so obliging that he placed the whole, empty town at our disposal. It would have helped us more if he had been less obliging and had dictatorially provided us with one shop into which to stick the canteen and its confounded sutlers. And it poured, and we continued to wander about the empty streets. And it poured—and, in the most unexpected places, the disreputable Acting Lance Corporal in charge of Divisional Canteen would bob up, touch his cap like a London cab-runner and exclaim, always in three breaths: "Xcusemesir; may-I-speak-to-you-sir; have-you-found-a-billet-for-the-Divisional-Canteen-sir?" He was a most annoying person, a London music hall "turn" in peace time. He occupied his leisure moments behind the Canteen Counter in writing "sketches" for London Halls, like the Hoxton Empire, at fifty pounds a time.

Sometimes he would appear alone or would emerge alone from the chalk-rubbish and festoons of wall-paper of an empty shop. Sometimes he would have behind him a disreputable French country cart loaded with sardine tins, sticks of shaving soap, cigarette packets, cratesful of wet dates, writing tablets—God knows what. And the horse—or it may have been a mule—seemed to be a hundred years old. And rain dripped from its ears. And rain poured on the disagreeable objects in the tilt cart and on the three impossible Tommies who went with it. And they would have backgrounds of black, wet houses, without roofs, but with lace window curtains dripping in all the empty window spaces; and wet, smashed chairs and commodes and wardrobes hung drunkenly over holes in the floors of houses that had no front walls. And it poured. And twilight deepened.

Then a battalion came in along the Bailleul road; a poor, smashed battalion, with men limping and men under whose tin hats there gleamed white bandages, very conspicuous in the rain and the mud and the dark, wet khaki. And a battalion looks grim indeed when it has been hammered by artillery, on a Macadam road without chance of retaliation—owing to a blunder of a staff officer. They had, I think, 160 men killed in one company—pretty well the whole strength as battalions were in those days. I don't like to think of it, much.

And yet, such is poor human nature, that both I and my companion said, "Thank God!"—as we had never said, "Thank God" in our lives before. At least I know that I said "Thank God" as I had never in my life said it before—and as I never shall again. For it wasn't our battalion that had been smashed by direct shell-fire on the Macadam road—Loire—Dranoutre—Neuve Eglise—Plugstreet—Nieppe. Imagine such a route—in full view of the Hun trenches! Why, riding that way the day before, to prospect next day's billets, I and another officer had had three shells directed to us alone by the German artillery—between Dranoutre and Neuve Eglise! So imagine what it would be for a battalion. And we had seen orders which said that *our* people were to leave Loire at such and such an hour and to march by Companies—presumably in column of route!—in the Dranoutre-Neuve Eglise-Plugstreet road! And the Divisional Transport Officer had told us early in the afternoon that, as we had *known* would be the case, our battalion had been hammered to pieces. A whole Company had been wiped out on that road—marching in column of route.[1] "A" Company, he had said, our own company!

Half the time during the afternoon, the other officer and myself—soaked to the skin and pestered by the farcical Lance-Corporal in Charge of Canteens—who, poor devil, was only doing his duty—had said, from horse to horse: "I wonder if Johnny A— has gone west! I wonder if Fred B— has copped it! . . ." It is horrible, that!

And then, in the rain, under the castle wall, we heard from a very bleeding man of the other Battalion that our own people, after all those of the W— Regiment had been murdered, had been diverted from the Dranoutre-Neuve Eglise road to the Locre-Bailleul-Armentières highway, which was, in those days, as safe as a church.

So we two, watching the men of the other Battalion march resentfully by, could say "Thank God" to ourselves.

Relief, naturally, manifested itself in the two of us, according to our separate temperaments. My friend—

[1] This would mean that the Company presented, as a target to the German artillery, a solid and slow-moving cube of human flesh 240 ft. x 8 ft. x 6 ft. *No* gunner could miss it.

he was an Irish Nationalist, almost a Sinn Feiner—said:

"G . . . , old dear. You're Division. I'm only Battalion. The canteen is your job. I think I'll get to my digs." He added, a bit bashfully, that in his digs there was a French girl who was going to give him lessons in her difficult tongue. I said, "All right. 'Op it." [I remembered saying ' 'Op it!' in an intense weariness.] But, as I turned my tired old horse once more down the road to find a billet for that accursed corporal of Divisional Canteen, I was, I remember, thinking innumerable things, all at once.

Firstly: my shirtcuffs were very frayed, and the rain had made them more diabolically wet and cold than you can imagine. Then I was actually bothering about the wretched staff officer who had murdered all those men. I was worried about him. You see, it would be such a trifling thing to do—as easy as forgetting—as every human soul has done in its day—to post a letter. He would have an ordnance map and a pencil. The map would show the contours, but probably it would not show the German trenches or the German artillery emplacements. He would rule a pencil line from Locre to Armentières, he would see that the Dranoutre-

Neuve Eglise road was nearly level, running indeed along the flat at the edge of Flanders. On the other hand the Locre-Bailleul-Armentières road went up steeply from the Belgian frontier to Bailleul—a road in the dusty sunlight, the rough unshaded country, between tobacco and grain fields. And it was 1500 yards longer. So, in the kindness of his heart, he had saved the men the extra distance, the shadelessness, and the dust of a road over the foothills bordering Flanders. He had forgotten the Hun artillery—*just* as you or I might forget to post a letter!

And, as I rode past the workmen's villas, for the hundredth time, I was imagining that poor Acting Assistant Brigade Major, with his pink cheeks and his red hat, being strafed to hell by our frightful General of Division. He might almost cry! . . . But I daresay it wasn't at all like that, really.

Anyhow, I was being dreadfully sorry for him. At the same time, I was trying—if I may use a professional novelist's word—to psychologize the German gunner. He wouldn't believe his luck. He *couldn't* believe his luck. He would believe it was some accursed scheme of the diabolically cunning English to discover his position. There, through his telescope, he would see a solid cube of wet-brown, moving slowly along a perfectly visible road. He would see it with his naked eye —a cubical caterpillar as large as a whole range of farm buildings. It would be incredible to him. No doubt he would ring up his immediate superior, and they would confer over the telephone. He would tremble for his battery. The English were no doubt drawing some sort of canvas wind-screen, camouflaged to look like a company, along that Macadam road. They would be trying to draw his fire so as to discover his position. Then they would blow his battery to hell with new, unimaginable High Explosive Shells, or mines, or anything. So he would fire—and see 160 men killed. "Drum fire," I think the Germans called it. The complete Company would be wiped out—a mark such as a German gunner would hardly dare to pray for in his dreams. And nothing would happen to him. Nothing. He would wait. But nothing!

Then he would thank the Creator. . . .

I don't know really what happened to me then. I have said that that deluge of a twilight seemed to last a thousand years. I was wrong: it seemed to last two thousand years. I remember meeting the Divisional Transport Officer out in an immense expanse of mud near an incredibly dirty farmhouse—in a sea of brown liquid that was supposed to be the Station Road. And I know that the field stank. It smelled unimaginably —though I don't know why a field should smell. I can still smell it.

The Transport Officer said that that was the field allotted to him by Division. He said to hell with the lake of mud. *He* was going to put the Transport on the Bailleul-Steenewerck road. He gave the number on the map, "R. 14," I think it was. I said I should take the field for the Divisional Canteen. There were, scattered—possibly floating—about it some Connaught huts that resembled Noah's Arks adrift in a sewage farm. The Transport Officer said all right. I fancy he was not interested in the Divisional Canteen.

As we rode slowly, again past the workers' villas, the Lance-Corporal in Charge of Divisional Canteen again waylaid me, springing up apparently out of the mud. He said: "Xcusemesir, may I speak to you, sir . . . I've fahnd a 'ouse be'ind the Ch'ch for the D'vish'n'l C'nteen."

I think I went mad at that point, and the Transport Officer rode slowly away. I don't remember what I said to the Lance-Corporal. I hope I never shall.

The trouble was that, in that town, there was a danger zone. For the last four days, the Germans had been shelling the church. From 6:00 P.M. until midnight, in their methodical manner, every quarter of an hour they had dropped a 5-9 shell into the sacred edifice. The danger zone was therefore perfectly circumscribed and perfectly definite. But, unfortunately for me, though I had been warned that there *was* an official danger zone, no one that I met knew where it was. The town marshal had gone; the Divisional Police who were already working typewriters in his office were our Divisional Police, not those of the Division that had gone too. They knew nothing about the dangerous area. And some Australian humorist had removed all the cautionary boards that should have surrounded the church and had grouped them round a large iron public convenience which was the chief architectural adornment of the main street. There they looked alarming but improbable.

It was therefore not to be thought of that the L. C. and his men should remain in a house just under the shadow of the church—for it was plain that, however big or however circumscribed the official danger zone might be, what the Huns were shelling was the church. We had been in the church in the course of the afternoon. It was a commonplace building, as far as I can remember, Byzantine of an eighteenth century type. But it was, in a way, rendered gracious by the enormous heaps of plaster and stone-dust that piled against the walls in drifts, so that it was as if sand dunes had invaded the roofless edifice. And, in the course of the dusk, shells had landed in all that rubble, constantly, no doubt regularly, whilst we were pursued by the L. C. round the church square, in the rain that had begun to fall just as the Huns began to shell. . . .

I daresay the reader will by now be tired of the Lance-Corporal in Charge of Canteens. I know *I* was. And I am uncertain what became of him. I daresay I could remember if I made an effort—but it hardly seems worth while. I know that four days later he was safely writing a music-hall sketch, in a tent, under a counter made of soap boxes, in a field just beyond the turning where the Plugstreet road leaves the chaussée from Bailleul to Nieppe; and I know that next night I got out of my flea-bag at about 2:00 A.M. and wearily walked for miles and miles in search of him and his sardine tins. The Huns had started regularly bombarding the town at that inconsiderate hour, and I know too that, when I did find him, by chance, wandering about with his disreputable cart and his four disreputable men, he said that a shell had gone clean through the upper story of the shop that they had commandeered. So I suppose that that night he had slept in the town. I can't remember.

I can remember interviewing the *Maire* a second time and that, because he was busy with some French staff officers, I had to wait some minutes—in a dentist's waiting-room, with aspidistras, black walnut furniture, and innumerable copies of the illustrated paper called *Excelsior* on the lace table-cover. For the *Maire* was a dentist. He was also a brave man. I can remember, too, being in a shop just under the church where a young, stout Belgian Jewess was standing waist deep in remnants and rags of black satin. She was nonchalantly packing this away in sacks whilst I tried to make sense out of her middle-aged, frightened father. I think I was telling him that seven francs a day was too much to expect the Division to pay for the rent of a rag and bone shop. Something hit the roof at that moment and an avalanche of bones, old iron, and satin petticoats poured down the stairs from the upper floors. The father disappeared, exclaiming "Oi! Oi!" and elevating his hands above his bared head. But the daughter, with a large face, chalk-white with powder, heavy blue-black hair, and an opulent inscrutability—she had on her large white fingers a great collection of fat-looking wedding rings—went on nonchalantly examining black satin petticoats, rejecting some, folding others slowly, and packing them away in sacks. She seemed to regard the thing that had passed through the upper story with enigmatic indifference, as if shells and iron hail were just part of the silly vanity of the male sex. Her business was to pack up for transport on a barrow to Armentières all the black satin that she and her father had collected and that had once belonged to the inhabitants of the empty town.

That attitude seemed to be common enough in the women of those parts. I remember looking, five minutes later, through the bull's-eye glass of a cottage window so low that you would say every shell must pass over it. The interior was candle-lit and quite tranquil.

At trestle tables, gesticulating although they had their elbows on the boards, sat eight Tommies of the battalion whose entry we had witnessed. Five had bandages, and three had not. Between their elbows they had tinplatesful of fish and chips. And there were two women, standing. One, middle-aged and stout, had her hands on her hips, and her elbows back. Her blouse was well open at the neck, as if it had been hot work cooking the fish and chips. She stood against a trestle table and seemed to be giving back-chat to all the eight Tommies at once. The other was a young girl—of the Flemish Madonna type. Her yellow hair was tightly braided round her head; she leaned back against the mildew-stained wall, and on her bare, crossed arms she had a tabby kitten. It was biting her finger, and she stood entirely quiet, as if on her hands she had all the safety and all the time in the world.

I daresay it was safe enough for the moment. But, some days later, I noticed that there was no cottage there. There was not even a lace curtain.

I walked along—for I had got rid of my tired horse—a long way, under the dripping trees that were black above the wall of the château, and out onto the Bailleul road, a long way beyond the Plugstreet turning, I persuaded myself that I was going to ask the Divisional

Transport Officer to house my friends of the Canteen in tents in his field.

I found him in the W—— lines. They were eating Welsh rabbit and herrings in a Connaught hut. They were not pleased to see me. There was an old Quartermaster from Stratford-on-Avon—a butcher by profession, think of that!—who sat with his hands crossed over a large stomach and spectacles well down on his nose. Also he wore carpet slippers. He told me in a most businesslike way that they had only herrings enough for three. I was welcome to any amount of Welsh rabbit—but there were only herrings enough for three. And they were three already.

Then I realized that what I was really concerned about was to see my own Battalion come in. It was symptomatic. My friend the Sinn Feiner had been perfectly content, as soon as he had seen the W——'s come in and knew that our own people had been diverted, to go and take lessons in the language of the country from the French young lady whom he had unearthed. But, as for me, I wanted to *see* the Battalion. I had no particular reason to love the C.O. or the Sergeant Major. But I wanted to be absolutely *sure* that they were safe.

And, just as I got back to the crossroads near the church, the Battalion came in. There was the C.O. riding, the Sergeant Major walking ahead of him. And then "A" Company. I called out to Captain Gardiner, after I had saluted the Colonel: "A Company all right?" And the young man answered: "Cheerie Oh, old bird, as right as rain." The last dregs of light were fading under the elms; the Huns were putting in some extraordinarily heavy stuff just behind them. And suddenly I remembered that I had not billeted myself. God knows whom we hadn't billeted, the Sinn Feiner and I between us. Certainly three sets of battalion headquarters, transport, officers' messes, sanitary squads, and the men of a whole brigade. But I had nowhere to lay my head. And my frayed shirt-cuffs were streaming with rain and it had grown pitch dark. . . .

You say I am a poet. Certainly I am a poet!

And these eyes of mine that, when I have any leisure, see always not only the things that surround me, but many other things—these eyes of mine were busy. Certainly they saw what, in the darkness, was visible of the wet and stricken town. Against the sky the roof lines or the silhouettes of charred beams; the red glow of the candles in the fried-fish cottage; the red glow that slowly danced inside the church as if a black mass were going forward. I suppose the last shell had set fire to some woodwork. Then another came and put it out, so that it was darker.

But these eyes of mine that, with their attention, were looking at a bright landscape, had also registered in their memory a white, as if triangular patch, in a dark window of a house just behind the church, nearly opposite, but a little this side of the *Mairie,* a house that we had passed again and again. The eyes had noted that white luminosity and now made for it, though the thinking mind was differently intent. This sort of definition is a little difficult to make. Try to follow me. The department of my eyes that led me—the Intelligence Department—saw the roofs and the black streets; the department which was influenced by my desires—for a meal, for warmth, for a bed, and above all for dry shirt-cuffs—was leading my steps toward the house that had the pale luminosity in the dark window. And, what I suppose you would call my mind's eye was occupied by a bright landscape. That is to say, I was definitely thinking about an August landscape.

You will say that it was the landscape I have mentioned so often—the landscape with the stream and the trees and the gingerbread cottage. But it wasn't. That came later. I suppose that at that time I wasn't tired enough to see it. Besides, I never saw that as if in bright sunshine or in the weather of any accentuated season—but always as just English country in just English weather, green earth in a diffused light under a July sky. . . . No, I was thinking of a billeting scheme. For, in the long ago—thousands and thousands of years ago—we used to do billeting schemes, round Manorbier and Penhally. And I think the one I was then thinking of with—as the prose writers say—laughter mixed with rain, took place at Penhally. It appeared an idealized Penhally, mostly hollyhocks and thatch, so wilful is the mind, though I remember every house of Penhally! Well: a great many of us went in the August weather to work a billeting scheme there. And an officer representing Division drove up in a Rolls-Royce and pretended to "confer" with us. He had a red hat-band and a golden lion and the beautifullest moustaches and the beautifullest white whip-cord breeches and *such* spurs! And such ladies in the Rolls-Royce, awaited him!

And he gave us the loveliest hints in a clear voice, with the far-away expression of one who knows his job but lectures in it too often. Certainly he knew his job—and he was a fine fellow!

We were to get hold of the civil power at once, or at least as soon as we had conferred with the divisional billeting officer. The first thing to do was to find out about the water supply. Then we were to group our companies round the pump if we could. If there were only one, we were to call a conference of Company Quartermaster Sergeants and give out the time when each Company was to draw water. That would then go into Battalion Orders. He said, with a little smile, that we were to remember to put Battalion Headquarters into the best billet—because C.O.'s liked that—and Company messes must be lodged in public houses or places where there was liquor. So that the men shouldn't get at the alcohol! Transport should, as a rule, be as far from fire as could be arranged, to avoid stampeding of horses; similarly with the Doctor's cart and the Battalion cookers. And, as a rule, the Company detailed for the Advance Guard next day should have the advanced billets if there were no likelihood of a night attack. But they should not be exposed to disturbance in the night, if possible, because they would have a hard time next day. Similarly the Advanced Guard of that day should be halted first and be in the rear, so as to get a good night's rest. He told us to remember those splendid words which used to be the shibboleth of every British officer—to the effect that the comfort and convenience of the men should be considered before every exigency save the necessities of actual warfare.

Yes: he was a fine young fellow—one of the Old Contemptibles, as he modestly, clearly, and rather absent-mindedly, enunciated all that sound, common-sensible, old-fashioned lore of the Army. And I remember every word of it. For instance, men of separate units or even of separate Companies of the same Battalion should not be billeted on opposite sides of the same street; the street should be divided in half, and one-half allotted to each Company or unit. (I remember pointing that out to my Sinn Fein friend in one of the miserable, battered streets of workmen's hovels in Pont-de-Nieppe that afternoon.)

But, though I had listened with all my ears to the Staff Officer at Penhally, my eyes, even then had been playing the trick of showing me Pont-de-Nieppe—just as at Nieppe in France they insisted on showing me Penhally in Wales. For, whilst I listened to him, I was seeing the time when I should represent Division and be, in the sunlight, young, with a beautiful moustache and a red hat-band and white whip-cord breeches, very full. And with *such* spurs!

So there I was, representing Division.

It hadn't been very like what I had pictured—and I had not had to bother about water supply.[1] I had enough water in the wretched, frayed wristbands of my shirt, as it seemed, to water a whole Battalion and the mules of the Transport! But, otherwise, the traditions of the Old Army had prevailed. Rudimentarily, no doubt, but still, they had prevailed. I had reminded the Battalion Billeting Officers to see that Battalion Headquarters had convenient buildings, that officers had charge of any civilian liquor depots; that Company cooker-cars had emplacements convenient for their men, and that latrines were not located near water supplies. Also, we had got into touch with the civil power. . . . Only, there were no ladies in my

[1] It is odd to think that Nieppe at that date was still supplied with electric power by underground cables that the Huns had not yet discovered, from Lille.

Rolls-Royce—and my Rolls-Royce was two very wet-kneed legs! And as for my shirt-cuffs . . .

I suppose they were most in my mind. For it is the most horrible of human afflictions to have wet shirt-cuffs! So that, when I found my orderly, not where I had told him to be—in comparative safety in front of the workmen's villas but in the shadow of the door of the shop where the Jewess had packed up the black satin petticoats, waiting devotedly, though the shells that missed the church went close overhead—he said:

"She's took all them petticoats on a barrer in sacks to Armentières," [1] I answered:

"You can fall out. Tell my batman that I've gone somewhere to get my d—d shirt-cuffs dried."

Nevertheless, he followed me. It was, you see, the pride of *métier*. Alas, that there should be no English for those words. He was my orderly for the day—just any orderly from headquarters. But I was his charge. If I had ordered him to fall out, no doubt he would have gone, against his personal will but in obedience to orders, to some sort of comfort that his pals would have prepared for him. I, however, had said, "You *can*

[1] His name was Private Partridge of, I think, the 6th Wilts.—a fine fellow, but not to be confused with Private Phillips of the 9th Welsh, who was my wonderfully good batman: (Note by Gringoire).

fall out." It was permissive and left the falling out optional. But he saw before him an obviously eccentric and probably benevolent officer—and it was his job to be able to tell my batman where I lodged myself. Also, it was contrary to King's Regulations for officers to go anywhere alone where there is any danger at all from shell or other fire. So, though he must have been uncommonly wet and hungry and tired, he followed me to the door of the house in whose dark windows I had seen the luminous patch—the forehead of Rosalie Prudent as she sat sewing, her head bent forward, in the twilight.

I don't know how it is: but from the moment when I first saw that highlight—and it had been certainly three hours before—I had been perfectly sure that that was what it was—the forehead of a quiet woman bending her head forward to have more light from the high window whilst she sewed in the dusk. In a way it was not what one expected: the town had been evacuated of its civilian population the Sunday before, when the Huns—as it seemed, for the love of God—started shelling the church just as it had emptied after benediction. And they had shelled from six o'clock till midnight; and every night since then, from six o'clock till midnight they had shelled the church. And they were shelling it now—eighty yards away. It was a desolate, and it seemed a stupid business. But no doubt they had their purpose, though it was difficult to see what it was.

That was how Rosalie Prudent put it, as she sat sewing my wristbands by the stove, in the wash-house. I sat nearer the stove, naked to the waist, the red glow and the warmth that came from the red-hot iron of the circular furnace being, I can tell you, very agreeable to my shivering skin. Opposite me sat the orderly drinking a bottle of Burgundy—which he had richly deserved. The steam went up from his wet clothes and was tinged red by the light of the coke. . . .

In the extremely clean *salle-à-manger,* with a high faïence stove of blue and white tiles, a colza lamp with a white globe, a buffet in the Nouvel Art style, of yellow Austrian oak with brass insertions; at a yellow oak table covered with a green velvet table-cover fringed with lace, sat my friend the Sinn Feiner learning the French that is spoken in Plugstreet from the niece, Beatrice Prudent. She was teaching him French by selling him handkerchiefs edged with lace in whose corners she had embroidered multicolored initials. In two very clean, lavender-papered bedrooms, upstairs, with white bedsteads, strips of carpet beside them on the waxed floors, with valises opened and showing works of devotion, altar vases, empty biscuit tins containing unconsecrated wafers of the sacrament, trench boots, gas helmets, tin hats—sat two padres composing their sermons for the next day. The Roman Catholic—for I heard him preach on it next day—was meditating on the doctrine of the Immaculate Conception. I don't know what the Presbyterian was writing about.

But there the house was, large, quiet but for the shells, kept spotless by the labors of Rosalie and her niece Beatrice, and, as yet untouched—just as it had been evacuated by the factory manager and his family, who had fled on the Sunday after benediction. In one of the roomy, very tall parlors there was, over the fireplace, a gigantic figure of the Saviour, standing in robes of blue, white, and scarlet plaster of paris, holding on his left arm a great sheaf of white lilies and resting one hand on the head of a very thin plaster sheep of, I should think, a Rhineland breed. That was perhaps why the owner of the house had not trusted to its miraculous intervention in favor of his dwelling.

He might have—for I heard the other day that the house remained intact until the 11/11/'18.

Rosalie profited—for, when the French inhabitants fled, the British authorities allowed Belgian refugees to take their places on condition that they billeted the troops. So perhaps it had been to protect her that the immense Bon Dieu waited! She deserved it.

She came from Plugstreet, of which town she had been one of the richest bourgeoises, her husband being the miller. She had had a large, roomy house, a great yard with stables and carts; she had had a wealthy, goodish, but possibly too jovial husband, two affectionate, dutiful, and industrious sons, and two obedient daughters. On Sundays she had gone to mass wearing a black satin gown, and, on her breast, a gold-framed cameo as large as a saucer. It represented a very classical Paris, seated, I don't know why, apparently between the horns of a lyre and stretching out one hand—which no doubt contained the apple—toward three grouped Goddesses in rather respectable Flemish *déshabille*. Mme. Prudent retained this work of art, but her wardrobe was reduced to two blue cotton dresses.

I gathered all this, whilst I dozed by the black iron

stove, from her conversation with the orderly. She spoke Flemish, and he, Wiltshire, but they understood each other. Of course, they used signs and facial expressions. The flames through the interstices of the stove poured upward to the dim rafters of the washhouse roof, and, by its light, Mme. Rosalie sewed as if she had no other pride and no other purpose in the world. For she told of the fate of her men and her womenfolk abstractedly and passionlessly; pride only showed itself when she talked of the state of the house in which she had found a refuge. From time to time she would say that if Mm. the Proprietors returned, they would find the floors waxed; the stair-rods shining, the windows polished; woodruff and sweet herbs amongst the bed linen in the presses, and not a speck of dust on the plaster-robes of the great Bon Dieu in the *salon de réception*. That was her pride. . . .

As for the rest . . . On the 18th of August, 1914, her man had been killed in the Belgian Reserve somewhere near Liège; on the 20th of the same month her eldest son had been killed in the Belgian regiment of the Guides. He had expected to have an excellent career in the office of an *avocat*—in Brûges, I think. On the 8th of November, 1914, her remaining son had been killed in the 76th French Regiment of Infantry of the Line. He had been chief clerk to an architect of Paris. Her daughters had been, one apprentice and the other chief saleswoman of a celebrated *couturière* of Liège. She had heard of them once since the Germans had entered the city. A Belgian priest had written to her from the Isle of Wight in December, 1914, to say that some nuns had taken in Aimée and Félicité. Those were the names of her two daughters. . . .

And at the moment she started up. She remembered that she had forgotten the potatoes for Monsieur—Monsieur being myself. So out she went into the black garden and returned with a tin platter of potatoes.

On it were ten tubers of which she weighed each in her hand inscribing what they came to on a slate—so that she might account to Messieurs the owners, on their return, for the potatoes that she had dug from the garden. Then she called her niece from the dining room to wash and slice the potatoes. She was going to give me an omelette with bacon and fried potatoes for my supper. She sat down again and went on, sewing and talking to the orderly.

She began talking of the interior of her house in

Plugstreet; she described minutely all the furniture in all the apartments. In each of the bedrooms there was a night commode in mahogany and a statue of the Virgin, also one of the Blessed Saints, and a *prie-dieu,* also in mahogany. . . . And now there was nothing. Every fortnight she was permitted by the British military police to visit her house—and she stayed there, in Nieppe, so that every fortnight she might revisit her house—which now, she said, contained nothing. The shells were shaking it to pieces. The tiles were all gone; the rain was soaking into the upper floors. The furniture was all gone—the great presses with her linen, the wardrobes—*en acajou*—which had contained her black satin dress and her husband's Sunday clothes. . . .

But she continued to catalogue to the orderly the contents of her residence. I don't know why it should interest him, but it did; for he nodded sagely when she talked of the *bahûts en bois de chêne,* and the immortels in vases on the piano. . . .

Suddenly she turned her head to me and said to me, where I sat writing with my tablet on my knee:

"And I ask you, *M. l'officier,* for what purpose is it that one brings men children into the world if this is to be the end? They cause great pain in their entry, greater than at the entry of little girl children. It is difficult to keep them alive so that they reach men's estate. And then it is difficult to keep them in the paths of virtue. And then they are gone."

XII

The Movies[1]

I WAS a little bewildered when Mme. Prudent so addressed me. For, to tell the truth, I had not been listening to her very attentively. She seemed to accept the war—this war, states of war, any operations that washed and disintegrated the interiors of the world—she seemed to accept them so tacitly as being part of the child's madness of the male that, in the warmth I had just dozed, not thinking much of her immense losses and not knowing at all that she would have anything very striking to say about the war. Besides, it was unusual to be beside a stove, under a roof.

And, when she had come in with the potatoes, out of the darkness, I had suddenly seen again that vision in green—of the sanctuary! And I remembered, extraordinarily, how once, years and years and years be-

[1] Gringoire particularly asks me to style this chapter as above because the Eminent Reformer, mentioned in Part I, Chapter VI, once said that the Writing on the Wall at Belshazzar's Feast was the first recorded instance of a Kinematographic production. It seems stupid: but our friend insists. He also asks me to say that Mme. Prudent's name was really *Dutoit*.

fore, I had gone digging potatoes at night. I suppose some visitor had come to my cottage late. And I had put my hand into the ground to take out a potato, and I found the earth quite warm. The air cools off quicker than the sod, you see, after a hot day. It had astonished me then—and, in that house, the remembrance came again, vivid and astonishing, for it had produced exactly the effect of one's having thrust one's hand into the breast of a woman. . . .

Well, I had been thinking of that and looking at that green landscape. And then, suddenly, I had pulled myself together. For it had occurred to me that I was not doing my duty. I had it in my head that I had got that soft, wet undangerous job of billeting, at the request of the bearded gentleman in the frock coat, who had sat under the picture by Bastien Lepage—or was it by Marie Bashkirtseff?—in front of the great table with the carnations and the miniature *Niké*. I daresay it was not the fact: or it may have been. There is no knowing. In France you were taken up, like a brown paper parcel, and deposited here or there at the behest of two obscure lines of smudged typewriting in some one's Orders. And you did not know why; you had no will.

So I felt that I ought to be writing. It would not be fair to have a soft job for the purpose of wooing the Muse and then not to woo her. So I had pulled out from my wet tunic which hung over the chair back, my disreputable and sodden tablet of writing paper, which I had purchased two days before from that miserable Canteen Lance-Corporal and had begun, with a wet stump of pencil, to write the article called *"Une Partie de Cricket"* which, if only because it is a souvenir, I hope will be printed as an appendix to these remembrances. I know I wrote the first ten sentences, because I remember them and also because, the other day, I turned out the repulsive flap of my camp bed, and there, along with a damp sock and some mildewed straps, was the mouldering tablet with three scrawled pages. . . .

But I couldn't keep on writing. I was obsessed with the idea of a country, *patrie,* republic, body politic, call it what you will—that the recollection of that minister had called up in me. Yes: I had a vision of a country.

In the center was the Ministry—like the heart of an onion—and all the others that I had seen in the last week went round about it. Mind you, I have nothing to say against that Minister. I may have appeared to speak of him sardonically: that is a habit I have. But he, or something like him, was indispensable to the higher strategy of his nation:[1] and this man knew his job. What he wanted was perfectly the right thing: and if he did not know that the First Line Transport of a Battalion in the trenches was not exactly the happiest place in which to write lofty prose—well, it is certainly hypocrisy to seek, in the heart of the Sacred Emperor, for a knowledge of low tea-shops. He did not, obviously, like me but I have not the slightest doubt that I appeared drunk to him. Only a drunkard, really, would seek for ferrets in the palace of the Sacred Emperor. Yet I had my excuse. First of everything in the world—of everything in the whole world! —comes your battalion. And the ferrets of my battalion had all died suddenly; and the last thing they had said to me had been: Don't forget to get us some ferrets. If you had seen the rats of Locre you would have understood.

[1] It should be remembered that the military description of "tactics" is the direction of troops when in contact with the enemy. "Strategy" includes the direction of all movements that take place outside the immediate firing line. The conversion of neutral nations into allies or the cementing of bonds between allies by literary manifestations is specifically and according to the textbooks a branch of strategy, so that Gringoire is using the correct military word.

But the Minister had not seen the rats of Locre so he had not understood. . . .

No: he was a good man, in the right place. And very properly he sat amongst the gracious products of a State art—the pictures, the tapestries, the ormolu, the august building, the frescoes, the great staircases. And attendants who looked like bishops must be there to answer his bell; and Suisses with their great cocked hats and immense white gloves and their sabres with silver scabbards. There must be symbols of the Temporal Power of the State, which is august, ancient, and fit to be upheld. And, in disturbed times, there must be Civil Police in the courtyard, for strange visitors will come. And sentries there must be in the tricolored sentry-boxes beside the *porte-cochère;* sentries to call out the guard. And famous battalions must pass the door, along the boulevard, now and again.

And, round the Palace of the Sacred Emperor, there must be the Great City, and round the Great City must be La Grande Nation—stretching away and away, for miles and miles and miles. . . .

It presented itself to me as twenty-seven hours of railway journey—past Etaples where I had spent, years before, long days in *châlets* amongst the pine wood;

past Calais where my grandfather was born; to Hazebrouck where, during the war, we had found the worst billiard table in the world and where, whilst we waited for a connection, a German plane was dropping bombs on the goods line and Cochin-Chinese in furred silk hoods were working as plate-layers. And so to Steenewerck, where the great farm carts and tilburies and berlins were mixed up with artillery horses, with timber wagons, with immense guns.

And so the land stretched out to Nieppe and the wash-house and Rosalie Prudent sewing in the light of the circular cast-iron stove that had become red hot. And on the stove there were bubbling the pots which contained supper for me and coffee for my friend the Sinn Feiner. And whilst Rosalie sewed, ever and again, the pots lifted themselves an inch off the dully red-hot disk and then sat down again. Shells, you see, were falling in the church.

So the land stretched out—yes, like a gramophone disk!—till it came to the wash-house that was intact amidst all the smashed houses with their forlorn lace window curtains. And all that edge of the disk was smashed houses inhabited by steadfast souls who sat sewing whilst the pots jumped on the hobs. They were the caretakers of *Messieurs les Propriétaires* who had fled. There was a whole population of them: I came myself across a whole population of these quiet people, who considered only their duties to absent proprietors amongst the *rain* of shells. I remember when I went to have lunch with the officers of our 2nd Battalion—all dead, the officers that I had lunch with!—in Albert, there sat and read the *Libre Parole,* such a very old caretaker. He had gray side-whiskers, a white apron, a yellow and black striped waistcoat, a square black alpaca cap or *bêret*—for all the world like an old domestic of a Paris nobleman's hotel. He sat there, his legs crossed, his head thrown back, reading the paper, through silver-rimmed spectacles at the end of his nose. On the table beside him were a bullfinch in a gilt cage constructed like a pagoda and his black leather spectacle case. He had nothing to communicate about the war, except, I am glad to say, that the officers of the battalion were careful of the furniture, but he was so busy that he could not keep the floors as cleanly waxed as he desired. He asked me if I could not speak to Colonel Partridge about it. The Germans were putting in their usual lunch-time shells into that street; he was sitting reading in a glass-roofed passage between the kitchen and the *salle à manger*. . . .

Yes: a host of such people came into my mind as I sat beside the stove. I am not going to talk about the war any more. By the grace of God, I will never talk about the war again whilst I live. As you say: the people who did not take part hate to be reminded of that part; and the people who did take part have had enough of it. Yes; you are right. I made the mistake of my life, professionally, *quand je m'en allais en guerre*. It got me disliked by the critics, and it is bad to be disliked by the critics—for a poet.[1] So you see, I too have my prudences.

And indeed I have my prudences—though they are not the prudences of other people. I do not desire money, glory, the praise of my kind whom I distrust, nor yet to dominate humanity, which is a beast that I dislike. I do not desire friends; I do not desire broad lands. So, thinking about things in the wash-house of

[1] As far as the compiler has been able to discover, the poet's only ground for this diatribe is a review that his last volume of poems received from the —— Literary Supplement. In this the reviewer devotes one line to saying that the volume of poems is the best that was published during the war and the rest to personal abuse of our friend—and that is all. Our friend says that this is not cricket. It probably is not; but one should never say so.

Mme. Rosalie, I said: "I must dig myself in." I said, indeed, twice: "I must dig myself in. . . . "

I must have a dugout, as proof as possible against the shells launched against me by blind and august destiny; round about it there must be the strong barbed wire of solitude and, within the entanglements, space for a kitchen garden. Do you remember, Mr. Compiler, the redoubt our regiment made once—Montgomery's Folly? There was the redoubt, a circular piece of engineering. Round about it there was a level space of fifty yards, to give a field of fire, surrounded by the apron of wire. And, in that level space, you remember, we made the Regimental Gardens. . . . Well, in the wash-house, I said to myself that, *appry la gair finny,* I must make for myself, in space and time, an affair like that, or as like it as possible. If I could afford a cottage, I would have a cottage: if not, any sort of shelter made of old tins filled with clay with a bit of corrugated iron for a roof, a door of sacking, a groundsheet for carpet. As for furniture, aren't there bully-beef cases still? . . . *You* remember!

Lord! the interiors we have constructed out of such materials and the fun we had. And how they vanished like a drift of leaves when we were drafted away.

And how solid they seemed and work we did in them whilst they lasted, those interiors! So, I said to myself, in Mme. Rosalie's wash-house, I shall get along somehow. And then, said I to myself: There is the question of food.

Well, there is gardening! As you know, I am not *le dernier venu* when it comes to gardening. I will back myself to get twice as much off any given piece of ground as any ordinary man—if you will give me some seeds and a bit of old iron and a stick capable of being tied together into some semblance of a hoe. . . .

So the war finished for me, looking at Mme. Rosalie as she sat entirely engrossed in her work whilst the shells made the pots jump alive off the red-hot iron plate. . . . The war was finished, since my line was taken for *appry la gair finny*. That we should win I had no doubt, for, though the horrible scalawags who wangle themselves into notoriety had too much to say in the world, our heart was in it, and the heart of the other side was not. I knew enough to know that. If God were good to one, for one's self personally, it would finish there. I did not even want to stay to see the finish: I was so certain that we should win. But I had been worrying a little about myself. I couldn't, you see, see anything but the workhouse for me, if I lived through. And, at my age, the workhouse is not a pleasant thought. I am just too old, and just too young for the workhouse.

But the spectacle of Madame Rosalie, fetching in the potatoes, saved me. . . . I will tell you an odd thing. I have spoken of the recumbent oval of green light that now and again had appeared to me, to turn into a picture of a green valley. I will confess that, hitherto, I had feared it. It had come into my head that it might be a symptom of a seizure, an epileptic fit perhaps, or of some obscure but disastrous nervous disease. *Ker vooly voo? Say la gair*. That region of the world had its trials for the nerves of people of my age. One might well be on the edge of something.

But looking at Mme. Rosalie—so extremely centered in the work in hand, so oblivious to the very real danger, so brave and so tranquil, I said to myself:

"What the devil! If she can stick it, I too can!"

For what had she to look forward to? She had said that, on the last occasion when the British authorities had permitted her to visit her house at Plugstreet they had not allowed her to enter it. The front wall of the upper part had fallen inward and for her sole possession she could see that on the wall of Félicité's bedroom that was exposed to the sky, there hung a gilt-framed Souvenir of her daughter's First Communion. Nothing else! Nothing! That was her sole possession in the world except for two gowns of blue Manchester goods and the cameo that represented the judgment of Paris. . . .

And suddenly I was convinced that the apparition of that recumbent green oval was, not a visitation, but a sign. If from that time onward I just carried on, if I persevered—as I was truly minded to persevere, in my duties as a poor bloody footslogger—the Almighty would give to me at least sufficient space in the quiet earth that was just country—to dig myself in. Well, God has been good to me, as you see.

And, mind you, I consider and consider proudly, that I am doing, most of all, my duty to the State. I have always considered myself a member of the governing classes, with the privileges and the duties. And I abate nothing of that opinion. It seems to me to be my duty to govern, if not by directing, then at least by guiding, through the superiority of my insight. I am not fitted for the intrigues of what is called Public Life. No doubt that is no worse today than it was in the time of Alcibiades or the late Mr. Gladstone. But it is very bad; very vile.

You say: how do I presume to speculate on public matters who cut myself deliberately off from the consideration of public matters on the 8/9/'16? My friend, I have considered the public matters of the 8/9/1816; of the 4/9/1870; 1770; 1470; of the 8/9/'16 of B.C. 1070. And there is no difference. If it is not an hypocrisy, it remains still a very wearisome matter to search for the person of the Sacred Emperor in a low teahouse. Well, I have done my share of searching and am too old for any more.

I have said that there is no difference between the public matters of today and those of the day of Alcibiades. But there is one very great difference: there is the difference that today—and it was never the case before—all the ground of the world that is capable of growing wheat is occupied by wheat and the population of the world is increasing by leaps and bounds. I will tell you: Some years before the war I was in a little town on the coast of France not far from Dunkirk. And my hotel was full of affrighted women; of nuns whose convents had been burned over their heads; and of ruined, wounded, and despairing men from the Low Countries. St. Quentin had been sacked; other towns were afire. A year before you could read in the papers the despatches of intrepid war correspondents in the South of France. They wrote from hotels—just as they did a year or so ago—how towns were flaming, streets running with wine, how the 5-9 shells soared and the naval howitzers raised their muzzles and coughed. You know the sort of thing!

Well! Those were the fingers on the wall. They were merely food-riots but they predicted Armageddon for those that can read—and still they predict an Armageddon beside which that in which we all took part was one of Gilbert White's rush candles against the searchlights of a battleship. Those were food riots, caused by the determination of town dwellers to enforce prices on peasants. The last war was a food riot: the next war will be a food riot beyond the imagination of the sons of men.

Nothing can prevent it or much delay it unless there should come a change in the hearts of humanity. And I do not perceive much change in the hearts of man—and all the wheat-land of the world is occupied by wheat and the population of the world is increasing by leaps and bounds. *Mene, mene, tekel, upharsin!*

You say that there are revolutions on foot. There always have been. But they have always been *révolutions de palais* and *révolutions de palais* they will always remain. What does it matter to me or to any sane man whether it is the Duke of Omnium or Mr. Evans of Llanfair-Rhaiado, or Mr. Hicks of Poplar who sits in the seats once occupied by Sir Robert Walpole or Mr. Jonkinsen or Colbert or Caius Julius Cæsar? None of those departed statesmen had to face the problem of a globe whose wheat-land was all occupied and whose population was increasing by leaps and bounds. In consequence they were not so greedy for money, or for the jazz bands of excitement that may make them forget tomorrow. For that is what it all comes to.

So I go out of public life of that type.

But don't believe that I, Gringoire, Hippolyte, de l'Institut de France, go out of public life! No, I go into it. For I go to prove that a decent life, clean, contemplative, intent, skilful, and with its little luxuries, may yet be lived by the Gringoires of the world—*hominibus bonæ voluntatis*. For, though I am a poet, it is thus that I interpret the message of the angel. For it is thus that I see the world—as a world of a few

Gringoires and of infinite millions that are the stuff to fill graveyards. I can't see it any other way.

And I said to myself in the wash-house of Madame Rosalie whilst some fragments of iron and rubble pattered down on the tiles of the pent-roof from the nearby church that, for the rest of my life I would be what I will call self-supporting—at any rate after the war was finished—and I will govern!

For I will be dependent on the profits of no man's labor, and I will produce more food than I eat and more thought than I take from the world. So, to the measure of the light vouchsafed, shall some fragment of the world be dependent on me. It is the only way to govern.

All this wangling for power in newspapers, meetings, market-places, and drawing-rooms is a weariness —and when you have it, what is it? A handful of dried leaves that crumble under the touch. If you have a platoon you can make it smart; if you have a garden, you may make it fine, luxuriant, producing marrows as large as barrels. Or if you write a poem, you must make it beautiful. Everything else is vanity.

I . . . I who speak to you . . . can house myself, clothe myself, discipline, entertain, and think for myself—and I can feed more than myself. As the old saying went: I can build a house, plant a tree, write a book, and beget a son. No man who cannot do all these things is fit to govern. He cannot govern—for I and the men who are with me, of good will, shall withhold his food, his clothing, his thoughts for his mind.

You may say, Mr. Compiler, that you who write falsehoods for the newspapers, who organize in offices the carrying of things on wheels, who dig in the bowels of the earth, and hammer on iron plates—or who take the profits of those who do these things—that you will govern, or inherit, the earth and the civilization of the earth. You cannot. If you withhold the labor of your hands or your minds—the world goes on. If I should—you would starve in body and soul—and in jazz noises!

In the end, I think, the world will be driven to become a great beehive: there will be the workers who think of nothing but their work. They will think nothing of the profits. And there will be the drones who provide the jazz noises and the wheels—and who will be killed off from time to time.

That is what I have gathered from the ruined houses in Flanders and from the aloof quality of the faces that came back to me whilst I sat dozing and Rosalie Prudent sewed. The faces were those of the Lincolnshire Private, of Lieutenant Morgan, of Henri Gaudier, and of the caretaker in the house at Albert—and of the Quartermaster of the Wiltshires.[1] But, so that you may not think that I limit myself to one class of society, I will add the faces of Lord Kitchener, of Sir Edward Grey, and of the French Minister, whose name I have forgotten. I did not need to see in imagination the faces of the orderly or of Mme. Rosalie, for they were with me.

You will object that I single out for salvation in Gomorrah only those of whom I have talked. Certainly, it is only those that I single out—those of that type, for those, for me, are the *homines bonæ voluntatis* who must be preserved if the State is to continue. They have rather abstracted expressions since they think only of their work; they have aspects of fatigue, since the salvation of a world is a large order, and

[1] *Note by Gringoire.* I do not know why I am haunted by the remembrance of this man. He was killed by the direct hit of a shell. When I last saw him, he was reading a paper with the spectacles at the end of his nose like the caretaker at Albert. His tunic—with ten ribbons!—was open over his fat stomach, and he wore carpet slippers. He was as brave as a lion and as simple as a sheep: no soul then alive knew his job better. He was a butcher of Stratford-on-Avon. If he have left a young son, may the shade of the Divine William guide that young son's footsteps gently and humorously through the ways of life!

they bear on their backs the burden of the whole world; but they look at you directly, and in their glance is no expression of pride, ambition, profit, or renown. They have expressions of responsibility, for they are the governing classes. Others will have that title in the newspapers—but they govern only those who make the noises of jazz-bands. The food supply and the supply of poetry is in the hands of the Gringoires.

Buzzing noises make the world pleasant; it would be a grim and silent world without them. I should not like it, nor would the other Gringoires like it. It was in Coventry Street that I last met Lieutenant Morgan-Gringoire. But, from time to time the buzzers must be killed off. Destiny is remorseless: either those who buzz must die in occasional crowds or those who live to give food and poetry must go starve and the others with them. Destiny is remorseless.

But destiny is also just. The drones of the hive have a good time—and give a good time. Moreover they make splendid soldiers of the type of the Cockney or the Parigot. That, perhaps, is how destiny means them to get killed off. So they will have their good times; and they will also have glory, the glory of finding the person of the Sacred Emperor in some such low tea-house as was the Bois de Mametz on the 14/7/'16 when the 38th Division was murdered.

And maybe that is the best glory of all. God forbid that I should say it is not. And I like to think that, along with the good time that they had and the glory of standing in the presence of the Sacred Emperor, they found also—sanctuary. For I like very much to remember the smile that was on the face of Lt. Morgan when they dug him out from under the dirt of the communication-trench.

Do you remember the old Catholic idea that a man may find salvation between the saddle and the ground? Well, we know little of death—nothing of death. So I hope it is not a heresy to think that, as the eyelids of those who fell closed on their glory, they had long, long visions, like that green vision that came to me from time to time. For time is a very relative thing; and may they not well have had long, long illusions, seeming to last for years and years?—to the effect that they had found, each his imagined sanctuary, where there was the gingerbread cottage that, hand in hand, on tiptoe with some Gretel, they explored, crossing their fingers and crying *"Feignits"* in the face of destiny—and where the Hou-Hou-oo of the wolf upon the Montagne Noire shall sound so very distantly as to be only the comforting reminder of the Grimm we knew as children.

——Something like that.

That is all I have to say about the war, here and now. But you have poked your sardonic fun at me from time to time, Mr. Compiler, and though bargaining is no part of my nature, a determination to have my own way was born in me as pawkiness was in you. And now, I say this:

"You have poked your fun at me as writer and as cook, and decorated with only those attributions of yours—as if each of those little, half-concealed smiles were a rag and tatter on my shining-seated *pantalons,* you propose to exhibit me to your public. Well, you shan't except on my own terms. The first is that, as you have spoken of me as writer you should enshrine —like a shining fly in amber—in the gum of your lucubrations a specimen of my own writing as it came to me, precisely, in Nieppe. And the second is that, since you began this compilation with what purports to be an account of my entertainment of the guests who honor this lowly roof of ours, you shall, as truthfully entertain your readers—as truthfully as you can, for God gives to some of us vision and to some the gift of recounting things askew for the entertainment of those wider of mouth than of intelligence—you shall then entertain your readers with an account of the dishes which since early morning I have been preparing for the evening degustation of yourself, of my dear Sélysette and your friend Mrs. Carmody. For I observe that, though you poke fun at my hospitality you are not averse from begging your dimity madams to share what you have called, I think, our rough oaken board."

Mrs. Carmody was no more than the wife of the Headmaster of the King Edward VI Grammar School where your Compiler gives lessons in the English language and drill, in the neighboring town. She had expressed an urgent curiosity to witness the domestic felicities and the supposedly eccentric habits of my friends. For it is not to be imagined that a figure so marked as that of our poet could conceal itself in an isolated dingle of a Home County without setting a considerable part of that county agog with curiosity —any more than it is to be imagined that an usher in a diminutive but immensely ancient public school could forever stave off from contact with his most intimate friends the young and agreeable but still imperious wife of his Head.

But to the alarmed, but only half-expressed remonstrances of your Compiler—for what, he wondered would Gringoire insist on inserting into his pages; and wouldn't his patiently prosecuted work when, if ever, it saw the light, wouldn't it have the aspect of a mere rag-bag? To these alarmed, if only half-expressed remonstrances, Gringoire, arising to his lean, gray height, announced his immutable programme for the day. It was by then towards four of a very hot, but fast cooling, July afternoon. The sunflowers drooped on their stalks, flycatchers made their curious, interrupted flights into the shining air and back to the old roof. The cows from the meadow had crowded to the other side of the quickset hedge, and, rubbing themselves unceasingly to get rid of flies from their backs made a curious sound like the tearing of thin paper interspersed with the deep, tranquil sighings of their breaths. It was in short an English July afternoon—a time when, if ever, men should sit and ruminate in quiet.

But there was such a clamor! You would have said

that the itch of all the authors and all the regimental sergeants major had entered into our friend. Quick, the boy, dozing behind the house, must put in the mare and go to the station and see if the Bombay duck had come for the curry. Quick, the maid must bring tea half an hour before that diminutive creature was accustomed to bring it. Or, no. . . . She must put back tea an hour and Madame Sélysette must with her own incomparable fingers blow three quarts of shandygaff and not forget the lime-juice. And Madame Sélysette must find the article he had written at Nieppe, and must put out paper and pens and cut two quills just as he liked them and come down and entertain Compi—your humble servant the compiler—and see that no wasps had got under the cabbage-leaves that covered the syllabubs in the spring and see that the boy did not take the traces up two holes too short and . . .

Madame Sélysette put her charming and provocative bust out of the little square window space above and to the left of the porch.

"You propose to write, my friend?" she asked. "But you swore this morning that you would send me to Coventry for a week if I did not goad you into picking the greengages. . . ."

Gringoire made a sound like "Grrh", as if the Wolf of the Mountains had humorously snarled. He said: "You have no soul!" She made at him a little grimace and disappeared. But I could hear their endearments as they met on the sounding little wooden stairs and felt all the summer regrets of the nearly old bachelor.

There was however no rest that afternoon. It was well to have the great blue three-quart jug of shandygaff on the seat in the porch; it was agreeable to have Madame Séysette to one's self whilst she dotted a few of the 'i's' and crossed the 't's' as to the entangled career and theories of her great man—and there is no better drink of an English July afternoon than shandygaff that has a little edge of lime-juice given to it and that since dawn has had all its ingredients cooled in an ice-cold spring. And there is no pleasanter topic in the mouth of a gay and tranquil young woman assured of the adoration of her mate than her expressions of her humorous adoration for Himself and his crotchets. You reply that the adoration of a lively young woman expressed to yourself would be more agreeable, but that is not the case. For lively young women do not express adoration to the faces of their males; but, failing and replacing that, it is pleasant to sit in a porch and hearken to adoration of a roaring genius overhead. For it causes you to have daydreams of a time when you in revenge may sit in an upper room, with a lively young woman expressing to a third the adoration that she feels for yourself. . . .

But continuously our Gringoire's voice rumbled from inside his upper room. Then coming to the window he would shout:

"Sélysette Sé . . . ly . . . *sette.* . . . What is the colloquial English for . . ." Some phrase that I did not catch. Or:

"Sé . . . ly . . . sette. . . . *Est-ce que* . . ." And again something that I did not catch for my French is none of the strongest. But I should gather that it had something to do with his pots that were on the stove in the disreputable shanty that he called his cookhouse. For Madame would enter that erection like Eurydice disappearing into Orcus. Immediately would come the thunder of Gringoire descending the stairs as if he had fallen. He too would enter the cookhouse and there would be the sound of impassioned and farcical altercations. Then Gringoire would approach the porch with a face that resembled a beet root with the heat.

He would drink a pint of shandygaff at a swallow, exclaim:

"The stuff's bilge. . . . No, I don't mean the shandygaff. There is no one like Sélysette for compounding cold drinks. I trained her. I mean my prose. My prose is bilge. . . ." And he would thunder up the stairs whilst Madame tranquilly resumed her place.

Once she asked some questions about Mrs. Carmody and when I said that lady had the greatest possible admiration for Gringoire and even had some of his verses by heart she expressed amused relief. "For," said she, "there are going to be great storms and dinner won't be ready till ten."

It wasn't.

For, you understand, in the sometimes tranquil, sometimes tempestuous but always complex nature of my friend, the pride of authorship had for the moment come uppermost and he was determined to get *his* prose into his compiler's volume. But of late he had only written in French as he has told you. So he would come to the window and shout to me the question whether he would be allowed to insert his French prose. Without waiting for me to answer his question he would shout: "No, of course you won't!" and disappear. Then he would shout:

"But I can't translate my own damned stuff. In heaven's name what's the English for . . . The beastly colloquial English. . . ."

Towards seven, just when I was thinking that I must go and tidy myself for the approach of Mrs. Carmody, he appeared before me, dishevelled and with a mess of written papers dangling from his hands.

"Here, you," he exclaimed, "get your reporter's notebook and come with me!"

And, at the bottom of the garden, under the hedge beneath the damson trees he made me lie down in the grass which was there long and began to dictate to me. He couldn't, as he said, translate his own French prose because his own French was near his heart and his English much less. You might say that his passions were for English countrysides and for French prose and here the two met to his confusion. Perhaps it is impossible to interpret French prose in the long grass beneath an English quickset hedge.

In any case Gringoire was distracted as he dictated and I was distracted, using a shorthand that I almost never employ to take down his words that he whispered or shouted or intermingled with ejaculations that I was not intended to record. . . . And I was the more distracted because at the top of the garden I could see Mrs. Carmody and Madame Sélysette carrying implements and provisions for the dinner from the house door to the little platform beneath the enormous oak that overshadowed the spring. Those gay young things laughed over their burdens—for Mrs. Carmody, out of her School House, was at least as gay as Madame Sélysette. And every time that they laughed Gringoire, lying in the long grass, groaned and writhed with the whole of his immense length. I have relegated his French, for which he gave me the copy from some Swiss magazine, to an appendix. I can only hope that his French is better than his English version of it. But as to that I am no judge. I only wish that he had not insisted on my presenting an untidy book to the world, for in common, I believe, with most readers, I much dislike appendices. For when on a bookstall I see a book and, examining it, find appendices at the end, I think either that that is a learned work for which I am seldom in the mood, having studies enough of my own to pursue, or that the author is an untidy-minded fellow who has not given himself the pains to digest and put into his own phraseology matter that will almost certainly be tedious to read.

But in this case I have no alternative. The rages of Gringoire are things that I have no mind to face. Print his lucubrations I must or there would be the devil to pay. I am not certain that there won't be at least a minor fiend to propitiate as it is—I mean when Gringoire comes to look for his prose and finds it at the end of the volume.

There certainly was a tremendous row when he discovered that he had kept the ladies waiting. He howled with rage, sprang to his feet, rushed into his cook-house. . . .

And the first view that Mrs. Carmody had of a poet for whom, as you shall discover, she had a real veneration, was rushing along the face of the house towards the dinner-table beneath the oak. He was hatless, coatless, his shirt-collar was widely unbuttoned and he was bearing a huge tray covered with little saucersful of the piquant messes that he calls *hors d'œuvres.*

We dined.

I am, alas, no Brillat Savarin and Gringoire as cook is to say the least inarticulate. When he is not that he is profane. We had his *hors d'œuvres.* Then we had his curried lobster. What shall I say about his curry?

Do you know the sensation of suddenly leaving the level and swooping downwards on the little railways you get at Exhibitions or in fairgrounds? It is like that. You take your first forkful of one of Gringoire's inventions with misgivings mingled with anticipations. Then you are reassured. You say:

"This is at least supportable. I shall survive this."

You take a sip of his white wine. After that it flies.

But you can't *believe* in Gringoire as cook. . . . I sometimes wonder if even he believes in himself. I mean, I asked him the other day for the recipe for his curry, just as, at the beginning of this book, as I have reported, I tried to extract from him his directions for household management. The results were even more inarticulate. He said:

"Oh, you take any old thing—tinned lobster, bully beef, cold mutton. . . . And of course you fry . . . But curry powder is good for any dish. . . . Because of the garlic in it. . . . And which curry are you talking about? There are hundreds. The only thing that unites them is that the curry must be cooked. Don't you understand? The curry—the powder—itself must be cooked. For hours and hours. Do you see? No, you don't see. How can I remember what I put into the curry for your friend? Any old thing. . . ."

I know he hadn't put in any old thing, though it is probably true that the chief ingredient of his dish is his fine frenzy. But I remember the energy he had put into securing the fresh lobsters for that particular effort—and the special brand of French preserved oysters that he had had to have for his beefsteak, kidney and oyster pudding which on that menu followed the curry. The boy had been sent on a bicycle in one direction, Madame Sélysette and I in the dogcart to Ulpeston, he himself had borrowed a lift in the baker's cart and gone to Storrinton. . . . No, surely, not any old thing—though he surely believed what he said. . . .

At any rate towards eleven we were contented and he, appeased, sat back in his chair and talked about poultry foods to Mrs. Carmody, that being the first time that he had paid her any attention.

The great boughs of the oak in which there now hung three Chinese lanthorns—Madame Sélysette loves Chinese lanthorns—the great boughs of the oak towered quietly up towards the planets, great white moths appearing and disappearing again into the blackness around the glow of the lanthorns. The Dog-star hung low on the horizon before us and the owls called at ten-yard intervals as they flew along the little stream in the meadow. When they were silent the night-jar churned intermittently. When we too were silent the little tinkle of the stream from the spring made itself heard.

I think that Mrs. Carmody did not much want to talk about poultry though her white Leghorns had taken many prizes at County or even more important shows. I think she let the conversation drag purposely. For suddenly, when we had all been pensive for a minute or two, her voice said from the shadows:

" 'I should like to imagine a night . . . !' "

Gringoire exclaimed sharply:

"What? What's that? Don't!"

But Mrs. Carmody said defiantly:

"I will. Just to pay you . . . . To show you. . . ." And she began again:

" 'I should like to imagine
A moonlight in which there would be no machine
  guns!
For it is possible

The Movies

To come out of a trench or a hut or a tent or a
  church all in ruins;
To see the black perspective of long avenues
All silent;
The white strips of sky
At the sides, cut by the poplar trunks;
The white strips of sky
Above, diminishing—
The silence and blackness of the avenue
Enclosed by immensities of space
Spreading away
Over No Man's Land. . . .

For a minute . . .
For ten . . . .
There will be no star-shells
But the light of the untroubled stars;
There will be no Verey light,
But the light of the quiet moon
Like a swan.
And silence! . . .'"

The moon was at that moment just tipping over the ridge of trees before us. Mrs. Carmody hesitated.

"'Then . . . a long way . . .'"

The voice of Madame Sélysette said slowly:

" 'Then far away to the right . . .' "

Mrs. Carmody said: "Thank you!" and continued:

" 'Then far away to the right thro' the moonbeams
Wukka Wukka will go the machine guns,
And, far away to the left
Wukka Wukka
And sharply
Wuk . . . Wuk. . . . and then silence
For a space in the clear of the moon.' "

The impassive face of Gringoire that the moonlight just showed worked suddenly, the mouth just moving —oh, rather like a rabbit munching. He said:

"I wrote that in Nieppe in September 'sixteen. . . ." He added:

"And it's pleasant . . . you two remembering. . . ."

He reached out his right hand and took Mrs. Carmody's left, and his left and took Madame Sélysette's right.

" 'Rest,' " he said with his heavy tired voice, " 'after toil, port after stormy seas . . .' " He paused and added after a moment: " 'Do greatly please!' "

ENVOI

UNE PARTIE DE CRICKET

BEING A LETTER WRITTEN FROM THE LINES OF SUPPORT TO CAPITAINE UN TEL AT PARIS.

Mon cher Monsieur, Camarade et Confrère,

C'était derrière le bois de Bécourt, un soir de juillet, et nous étions en train de jouer au cricket tandis que les obus allemands passaient au-dessus de nos têtes. Les obus allemands arrivaient, semblant vouloir crier le mot anglais *weary,*—qui veut dire fatigué,—puis changeant d'avis, ils disaient—et péremptoirement—*whack*. Mais en jouant au cricket, on oublie l'orchestre boche: on n'entend plus les obus qui passent. Nous courions; nous adressions des objurgations au malheureux qui n'attrapait pas la balle; nous discutions même, parce que les règles du jeu de cricket—qu'on joue avec une balle de tennis, deux marteaux et deux caisses de *bully-beef*—sont un peu élastiques. La pelouse est d'argile, dure et cuite par le soleil presque tropical; en fait d'herbe nous n'avons que des chardons, pour spectateurs et pour barrières à la fois, les mulets de transport, alignés. Mais jamais le cricket international qu'on joue sur le terrain des Lords, dans le bois de Saint-Jean, n'a été si accidenté ni si émouvant que notre partie de cricket derrière le bois de Bécourt, ce soir de juillet. Nous avons crié, gesticulé, discuté, hurlé . . . nous, les officiers anglais, mornes, taciturnes!

Je vous présente ces considérations en forme de lettre, mon cher . . . j'aurais voulu plutôt écrire un essai, soigné, balancé, bien pensant. Mais il m'est impossible de ciseler de la prose ces jours-ci. "Que voulez-vous,"—comme disent nos Tommies,—"c'est la guerre!" J'ai passé vingt-cinq ans à chercher des cadences, à chasser des assonances, avec une rage acharnée, comme celle du bon père Flaubert. Mais aujourd'hui je n'écris que des lettres,—longues, diffuses, banales. L'autre affaire demande trop de temps, de loisir,—de chance!

Donc, nous étions en train de jouer au cricket, quand je vis passer tout près de nous un officier français de ma connaissance,—officier d'une de ces batteries de 75, admirables, et que, la nuit surtout, nous avons trouvées tellement réconfortantes, à cause de leur voix qui roulait sans cesse, à peu de mètres derrière notre dos. C'était un colosse gris-bleu, aux yeux bruns et sombres, à la moustache brune et lourde. Il restait là, campé sur ses jambes et sur sa canne, comme quelque instrument de guerre à trois jambes, silencieux et d'acier. Et quand je m'approchai de lui, il me dit:

—*I find that a little shocking. Very shocking!* (Je trouve ça un peu shocking. Même très shocking.)

Il regardait les joueurs de cricket qui continuaient à crier, à gesticuler et à courir entre les chardons gigantesques et les jambes des mulets dangereux. Je m'écriai:

—Au nom du bon Dieu, pourquoi?

Envoi

Il ne cessait pas de regarder les joueurs, et réfléchit longtemps avant de répondre. Et ce fut moi qui, m'impatientant, commençai à parler, et même à gesticuler. Je disais que nous étions nouvellement sortis des tranchées; que le jeu donnait la santé, remettait le moral, faisait oublier la guerre . . . que sais-je? Il réfléchissait toujours, et moi je parlais toujours. Puis enfin, il dit:

—*I find that this war should be a religion. On coming out the trenches one should sit—and reflect. Perhaps one should pray . . .* (Je trouve que cette guerre devrait être conduite en religion. En sortant des tranchées l'on devrait s'asseoir—et réfléchir. Peut-être devrait-on prier.)

Et puis . . . je parlai encore longuement sans qu'il répondît autre chose que:

—*I find that, all the same.*

Alors j'éclatai de rire. Car la situation me semblait tout d'un coup allégorique. Et si vous y pensez, mon cher, vous verrez pourquoi je riais. C'est parce que c'était lui, le représentant de Cyrano de Bergerac, qui parlait l'anglais et employait les monosyllabes d'un lord Kitchener de théâtre; tandis que moi, le représentant de tant de milords et officiers qui pendant tant de siècles n'ont rien trouvé de plus à dire que les deux syllabes "O . . . ah",—moi, qui aurais dû porter monocle et favoris jaunes, j'étais occupé à hurler et à mimer des phrases d'un français assez incohérent, comme un vrai Tartarin. Et tous les autres—officiers et O. R.—de mon régiment continuaient à sauter, à crier et à rire comme des enfants méridionaux.

* * * * *

Et, en vérité, le changement est étonnant et quelque peu émouvant. Nous avons toujours eu l'idée—tout le monde, même le Français a eu l'idée—que le peuple français, et surtout les officiers et soldats français étaient gais, débonnaires, loquaces, goguenards,—"bretteurs et hâbleurs sans vergogne." Eh bien, j'ai voyagé en permission de Steenewerck à Paris,—voyage qui dura dix-sept heures. Et, pendant ces dix-sept heures, quoiqu'il y eût toujours des officiers français assis dans les voitures, ou debout dans les couloirs du train, le voyage a été le plus silencieux que j'aie fait de ma vie. Personne ne parlait. Mais personne! Il y avait des colonels, des commandants, des capitaines. Et je ne puis croire que ce fût tout à fait de ma faute. Il est vrai que, partout dans le train, on lisait: "Taisez-vous; méfiez-vous",—et le reste. Mais c'eût été impossible que *tous* ces messieurs gris-bleus m'eussent attribué les oreilles ennemies dont parle l'affiche. Je portais l'uniforme khaki.

Non, certainement, le voyage n'a pas été accidenté. Je vais vous en raconter les incidents: de Hazebrouck à Calais cinq officiers français, qui n'échangèrent pas deux mots; de Calais à Abbeville, trente officiers. Je m'adressai à un capitaine d'artillerie, en grognant que le train marchait très lentement. Il me répondit en anglais:

—Many troops moving!

Et puis, silence!

A Amiens entre un monsieur en civil. C'était un samedi vers huit heures du matin, et le train avait l'air de ne vouloir arriver à Paris qu'après trois heures de l'après-midi. Comme j'avais des affaires à Paris et que je devais partir le lundi avant six heures, je demandai à ce monsieur si je trouverais les banques fermées, et les ministères, et les magasins. Il me répondit qu'il n'en savait rien, qu'il n'était pas chez lui à Paris. Il allait à Jersey pour prendre possession du corps d'une jeune fille qui, ayant été noyée à Dieppe, avait flotté jusqu'à Jersey. *Et lui aussi me répondit en anglais.*

Il commençait à pleurer tout doucement.

Et puis . . . silence; les officiers regardaient ce monsieur avec des yeux qui ne disaient rien. Mais ce n'était pas gai!

A Creil montent deux dames, jolies et bien mises. Elles ont assez parlé, ces deux-là. Croix-Rouge, œuvres de charité, colonels, familles! Mais les officiers ne les regardaient jamais. Pas un ne levait les yeux, quoiqu'elles fussent jeunes, jolies, bien mises. . . .

Tandis que, pendant le trajet de Rouen à Albert, nous autres—qui n'allions pas en permission!—nous avons chanté, parlé aux demoiselles qu'on voyait sur les perrons; joué au football le long du train; grimpé sur le toit des voitures.

J'exagère un peu, naturellement, ces différences. Ce n'est pas un article que je suis en train d'écrire, c'est une lettre. Mais je reconte quand même ce que mes yeux ont vu et mes oreilles entendu. . . . Et comment l'expliquer? Parce que ce n'est pas assez de dire—comme on me l'a dit assez souvent—que si, en Angleterre, les Allemands étaient établis entre York et Manchester, s'ils avaient saisi les industries, pillé les villes,—et fait ce que font les Boches!—nous aussi, nous serions tristes, mornes, silencieux. Je ne parle pas de la population civile de mon pays; je parle de gens dont la vie n'est pas gaie, qui sont expatriés, loin de leur patrie, et qui souffrent, je vous l'assure, d'une nostalgie très sincère. Car là-bas, sur la Somme ou en Belgique, l'on se sent bien oublié, bien abandonné, et très, très isolé, d'un isolement semblable à l'isolement de . . . Eh bien! c'est comme si l'on était suspendu—nous, quelques millions d'hommes!—sur un tapis, dans les infinitudes de l'espace. Les routes qui s'étendent devant nous cessent tout d'un coup, à quelques mètres, dans le *No Man's Land*. Et c'est bien triste à contempler, des grand'routes qui cessent tout d'un coup. Et puis les sentiers par lesquels on est venu—et qui s'étendent entre soi et son pays—sont des chemins que l'on ne doit pas traverser. . . . Et, tout comme un autre, l'on aime sa femme, sa maison, ses enfants, ses parents, son coin du feu, ses champs, ses fumiers, ses bœufs et ses bois. . . . Le soldat français a cela, au moins, qu'il se bat chez soi! Et c'est quelque chose pour lui, comme individu.

Je suppose que c'est pour oublier, non seulement les obus allemands, mais aussi celles qui nous sont si chères, le coin du feu où nous avons si souvent devisé, les champs, les fumiers, les bœufs et les bois,—c'est pour trouver "l'herbe qui s'appelle l'oubli", que nous jouons au cricket près de Bécourt, et sortons des tranchées en donnant des coups de pied à un football qui saute à travers les corps des hommes tombés, vers les Allemands. Est-ce faiblesse? Est-ce la source dont nous tirons ce que nous avons de fermeté, de hardiesse, de courage? Je n'en sais rien.

Aussi bien que moi, mon cher, vous avez connu la

difficulté de définir exactement et en termes justes les différences, les nuances des différences, qu'il y a entre des nations. Nous commençons par développer une théorie—et nous théorisons beaucoup trop tôt; ou bien nous prenons le contre-pied d'une théorie admise depuis des siècles. Nous avons eu en Angleterre les caricatures du dix-neuvième siècle, des guerres de Napoléon Ier, qui nous montraient le Français selon l'imagination populaire anglaise. C'était un coiffeur, mince et affamé, qui ne mangeait que des grenouilles. Et vous autres, vous aviez votre John Bull, gros comme un boeuf, le ventre grand comme le ventre d'un boeuf, et qui dévorait des boeufs entiers. Ou vous aviez le milord qui se suicidait par pur spleen. Elles étaient stupides, ces caricatures, mais il m'est impossible de croire qu'elles ne fussent pas sincères. Les Anglais qui s'étaient battus en France en 1815 avaient cherché ce qu'ils voyaient—mais ils l'avaient vu. De même pour les Français.

De même, peut-être, pour moi. J'étais venu d'une Angleterre émotionnée, couverte, de l'île d'Anglesey jusqu'à North Foreland, d'affiches patriotiques et coloriées, et puis, de la frontière belge jusqu'à Paris, j'ai vu une France sans affiches, grise, silencieuse, préoccupée. Mais pour moi il n'y avait rien de neuf à trouver la France préoccupée—parce que, pour moi, la France a toujours été la France des champs, des villages, des bois et des paysans. Et la France des paysans est une France bien laborieuse, qui travaille sans cesse entre bois et étangs ou sous les oliviers du Midi.

Et pour moi la population anglaise a toujours été un peuple des villes. Or, ce sont les habitants des grandes-villes qui, tout en travaillant aussi bien que vous voudrez, ont besoin de faire de temps en temps la noce—chacun selon sa nature. Et c'est peut-être là la raison—la *causa causans*—des différences entre l'armée française et nous autres. L'armée anglaise est une armée ouvrière, l'armée française est une armée plutôt paysanne. Des paysans, et surtout des paysans français, ont l' habitude de mesurer les sevérités, les nécessités implacables de la nature. Ils les confrontent sans cesse, pendant des semaines, des mois, des années. Ils ne peuvent y échapper,—ils ne peuvent pas s'évader de la contemplation des maux de la vie, des vents et des vers qui détruisent les récoltes, en prenant des jours de permission, en faisant des calembours, ou par cet "humour" âcre et plutôt triste qui est, peut-être, la qualité souveraine du Tommy anglais. Car inscrire sur un obus qu'on va lancer contre les Boches les mots *"Love to little Willie"* peut paraître stupide, shocking à des gens qui n'ont jamais été là-bas. Mais la psychologie humaine est très compliquée, et il est certain que la lecture d'inscriptions de ce genre sur les grands obus à côté desquels on passe le long des chaussées a beaucoup fait pour nous encourager quand nous avons avancé d'Albert vers La Boisselle. Pourquoi? C'est difficile à dire. C'est peut-être parce que, les obus étant terribles et funestes, voici un obus qui est devenu ridicule, joyeux, ou même humain. Car nous sommes tous anthropomorphistes—et qu'un seul obus puisse se commettre à être le véhicule d'un jeu d'esprit, cela suffit pour donner à des coeurs superstitieux l'idée que tous les obus peuvent être un peu moins surhumains qu'ils n'en ont l'air. Car on a peur des obus. Ce sont les messagers des dieux qui ont soif, qui se manifestent en sifflant, qui disent qu'ils sont fatigués, mais qui détruisent, en deux minutes, des villages, des fumiers, des champs entiers. De même pour la partie de cricket que nous avons jouée parmi des chardons couverts de poussière et qui cachaient les ossements des soldats tombés. C'était peut-être sacrilège, peut-être stupide.

Mais je vous assure, mon cher, que ce paysage de Bécourt, Fricourt, Mametz n'était pas joyeux. C'était en juillet, et le soleil laissait tomber ses rayons sur les vallées larges, sur la poussière qui montait au ciel, sur les pentes, sur les bois noirs. Mais cette terre ne riait pas! Elle s'étendait loin, loin; et sous l'horizon bleu-gris se trouvaient les terrains auxquels personne ne voulait penser. Non, la nature, là, semblait terrible et funeste—territoire où le Destin aveugle et implacable devait se manifester à des millions d'êtres. Et puis nous y avons joué au cricket—et tout de suite ce paysage funeste et surhumain est devenu . . . est devenu un champ de cricket!

Pour un intellectuel, un terrain restera un terrain, qu'on y voie en l'air des bombes, des obus ou une balle de tennis. Mais pour nous autres, un terrain où nous avons joué au cricket devient moins terrible, et nous y passerons nos jours avec plus de contentement, malgré les ossements des tombés qui se cachent sous la poussière des chardons énormes. C'est stupide, c'est sacrilège, si vous voulez. Mais nous sommes ainsi faits, nous autres qui sortons des grandes villes pour faire la guerre. Moi, je suis comme cela, j'ai senti comme cela, là-bas, derrière le bois de Bécourt, par un soir de juillet 1916.

Et je reste toujours votre affectionné,

G.

P.S. Et je vous prie de remarquer que toutes les personnes que j'ai rencontrées entre Steenewerck et Paris parlaient l'anglais. C'est déjà quelque chose.

THE END